Nick Carter dropped into a combat crouch,

holding the 9mm Luger at arm's length in both hands for accuracy.

The masked killer rounded the corner and came into range. Shouting wildly, he emptied the better part of a clip as he rushed the stairs. He threw plenty of lead but forgot to aim . . .

Carter didn't.

He squeezed off a well-placed shot and the masked man dropped. Blood bubbled out of his mouth as he brought up his gun. He looked very young where the openings in his mask bared his face.

He wouldn't get any older.

Carter gave him the coup de grace right between the eyes.

NICK CARTER IS IT!

FROM THE NICK CARTER
KILLMASTER SERIES

NIGHT OF THE CONDOR

KILL MASTER

NICK CARTER

JOVE BOOKS, NEW YORK

Dedicated to the men of the
Secret Service of the
United States of America

"Nick Carter" is a registered trademark of The Condé Nast Publications, Inc., registered in the United States Patent Office.

KILLMASTER #231: NIGHT OF THE CONDOR

A Jove Book/published by arrangement with
The Condé Nast Publications, Inc.

PRINTING HISTORY
Jove edition/November 1987

ISBN: 0-515-09255-X

Jove Books are published by The Berkley Publishing Group,
200 Madison Avenue, New York, New York 10016.
The name "JOVE" and the "J" logo
are trademarks belonging to Jove Publications, Inc.

PRINTED IN THE UNITED STATES OF AMERICA

10 9 8 7 6 5 4 3 2 1

PROLOGUE

Twenty years ago

The plane was flying through a mountain pass in the Peruvian Andes when it malfunctioned. There were three men on board: the pilot, the copilot, and the passenger who had chartered this night flight to Lima.

The little plane's single engine lurched, interrupting its steady rhythm. A dull booming sound shivered through the craft.

"My God!" the copilot said. "What was that?"

A red warning light showed on the instrument panel. The pilot threw switches and pressed buttons.

The fuel gauge needle twitched, wavered, then began a rapid drop. The engine sounded as if it were tearing itself apart.

The passenger shouted to make himself heard. "What's wrong?"

"Must be a fuel line break!" the copilot replied. "Smell that? It's gas!"

Raw, choking fumes filled the cabin. The engine sputtered, feathering the propellor. The plane lost speed and altitude.

The pilot worked the controls but couldn't stop their descent. He choked the engine and worked the flaps to prevent their speed from igniting the leaking fuel.

1

"No use," he said. "I'll have to take her down."

"Where?" the copilot demanded.

Titanic mountain peaks rose on either side. Below lay the desolate moonscape of the altiplano, rushing up fast.

"Can we parachute?" the passenger asked.

The pilot laughed grimly, shaking his head. "No time for that."

The ground neared. Eerie blue flames spread over the engine cowling.

"We're on fire!" the copilot shouted.

The pilot squinted through the window. "Wait—wait —I see something!"

"What?"

"There—dead ahead—looks like a lake!"

The moon was mirrored in a black pond that lay at the head of a long valley. As the plane dropped, the pond grew into a broad glacial lake. The view was obscured by fire and smoke from the burning engine.

"I'll try to ditch her," the pilot said in a flat, emotionless voice. "Radio our position."

The copilot spoke into a hand-held microphone: "Mayday! Mayday!"

There was no time to complete the message. The plane pulled out of a dive and swooped over the valley at a height of twenty feet.

The pilot skimmed the plane a few feet above the lake. The copilot babbled a prayer. The passenger, Colonel Edwin L. Dunninger, braced himself for the crash.

The plane hit the water.

A moment later, it sank from sight.

ONE

Now

A quarter-moon hung high over the Andean village of Santa Rosa when Father Benito Jaran returned from the countryside. He'd been visiting farmers who were too old or too ill to come to town.

The hour was late, the plaza was deserted, and the villagers had gone to bed. The homely, good-natured priest grinned as he anticipated the pleasure of resting his weary legs and dining on a bowl of hot soup. He picked up his pace as he crossed the cobblestones to his church.

Suddenly a flock of winged things burst out from under the eaves of a nearby building, startling the priest. Flying in spirals, they rose high above the town square.

Bats, thought Father Benito.

But they weren't bats, they were birds, and their numbers multiplied with every passing second, clouding the sky. The night was filled with their frightened cries as they fled Santa Rosa.

Dogs began howling all over town.

Dark windows filled with yellow light as villagers woke up.

The old iron bell in the church tower struck a single, hollow note.

It rang again, louder. The church doors were flung

3

open and the caretaker ran outside.

The priest called his name: "Hernando!"

"Father Benito!"

"I—I thought you were ringing the bell!"

"It rings itself, Father!"

"But how . . ." the priest gasped, as the bell rang for a third time.

Thunder crashed, not in the sky but from underground. Father Benito reeled as the plaza rippled.

"Earthquake!" Hernando shouted. Fighting to keep his balance, he hurried the priest out from under the shadow of the church and into the open.

People clad in nightclothes fled their houses.

The plaza tilted, rising and falling like a restless sea. Windows shattered. The streets were pelted with roofing tiles and pieces of masonry. The church bell rang again and again.

Santa Rosa was slammed by furious noise and vibration.

The fury weakened. The earthquake died down and faded away. A few mild aftershocks marked its passage.

Then it was over, finished as suddenly as it had begun.

Father Benito let out the breath he'd been holding. "The Lord be praised!"

Stunned villagers gathered around him and joined him in prayer.

Travel is hard in the rugged Peruvian highlands. A day passed before Father Benito learned that the tremor that rocked Santa Rosa was only a minor by-product of a massive disturbance that struck the windswept plateau twenty miles west of town.

Herdsmen from that remote region sent runners to town to tell the priest what the quake had unearthed.

TWO

Julio Gallardo was puzzled. "An earthquake drains a lake in the altiplano. A wrecked plane is found on the dry lake bottom. The first reports identify the plane as one that vanished twenty years ago."

"It's no ordinary plane," Pedro Morales said. He was the managing editor of *La República*, one of Lima's daily newspapers. He was a thin man with tired eyes who looked ten years older than his age of forty-five.

Gallardo, the paper's owner-publisher, was well fed and robust. "What makes this plane so unusual?"

"It was carrying a *norteamericano* named Dunninger," Morales said.

"So?"

Arturo Fernandez, Gallardo's assistant, chimed in. "We did some checking. This Dunninger was a big man in the CIA. He was very well connected politically, with influence in the highest echelons of the United States government."

"Interesting," Gallardo yawned, "but of academic interest only, since it turns out that the plane was mis-identified. It wasn't the one that was lost twenty years ago. It was a geological survey plane that was lost five years ago."

"We think otherwise," Morales said.

"That wasn't what you said two days ago, when you

5

ran a correction to the original story. What made you change your mind?"

"Two days ago I didn't have this." Morales tapped a fat folder on his desk.

Gallardo came around to the back of the desk and looked over Morales's shoulder as the editor spread the folder's contents on the blotter. The material included typed statements, Xeroxed logbook entries, flight plans, manifests, and photographs of both intact and wrecked aircraft.

"Quite a package," Gallardo said. "But what does it mean?"

"It proves that the wreck was Dunninger's plane. It also proves that Inspector Chamorro of the Bureau of Aeronautics was lying when he certified it as the geo-survey plane."

"Or just honestly mistaken," Gallardo suggested.

"Then why won't he answer our phone calls?" Fernandez shot back. "Why won't he consent to be interviewed? These are hardly the actions of an honest man with nothing to hide."

"Nobody likes to admit he made a mistake," Gallardo pointed out, "especially not a bureaucrat."

"There's more to it than that," Morales insisted. "Somebody doesn't want us investigating the story."

"Ah-hah!" Gallardo showed his first signs of genuine interest. "Tell me more."

"After I assigned Gomez to follow up the story, I received an anonymous telephone call here at the office," Morales said. "The caller said it would be healthier for all concerned if the investigation were dropped."

"I like that!" Gallardo smacked a fist into his palm. "I like that! I know one thing—when somebody warns me off a story, that story is worth covering!"

"I was hoping you'd say that," Morales said.

"Nobody pushes *La República* around!"

Gallardo went to the window and opened it. "Let's get some fresh air in here."

The office was thick with stale, smoky air. Gallardo stuck his head out the window and took a few deep breaths. The night air was stale and smoky too.

Gallardo stalked back to the desk, briskly rubbing his hands. "Where is Gomez? He should be here. After all, it's his story."

"He's trying to track down the elusive Inspector Chamorro," Fernandez replied.

"He really hasn't started digging yet," Morales said. "We were waiting for you to give us the go-ahead."

"You've got it," Gallardo said.

"Great!"

A muffled shout came from outside the office.

"What was that?" Gallardo asked.

The trio listened, but the noise wasn't repeated.

Fernandez shrugged. "It must have been the custodian or the watchman. They're the only ones in the building besides us."

"They're probably fooling around instead of doing their jobs," Gallardo muttered. "We won't make that mistake."

He examined some of the documents on the desk. "Impressive. That Gomez is a reporter who does his job."

"Gomez didn't collect this information," Morales said.

"He didn't? Then who did?"

"I wish I knew. The package was delivered by a messenger who left before anybody questioned him. I doubt that he knew the identity of our mysterious informant.

Whoever that person is, he's methodical and smart —too smart to give himself away."

"I'm not sure I like this," Gallardo said. "You know what they say about Greeks bearing gifts. Maybe it's a plot by one of our competitors to mislead us into making fools of ourselves."

"The source is unknown, but the information checks out. It's no hoax," Morales said.

Gallardo stroked his chin thoughtfully. "It seems we have two forces in conflict. The side represented by our anonymous tipster wants the cover-up exposed. The other side wants it to remain a secret. But what makes a twenty-year-old plane crash so important to either side?"

"That's what we've got to find out," Morales said.

"You already know too much, señor."

The newsmen gaped at the intruder who had just spoken.

He was a small, spindly man with a head too big for his body. He held a pistol in one hand and a briefcase in the other.

His partner followed him into the office. The second man was a six-foot-six powerhouse with a cruel face. He was well groomed and fashionably dressed. His huge hands held no weapons. They were his weapons.

Morales was the first to recover his wits. He was angry, not afraid. "Who the hell are you?"

"You don't know me?" The small man pouted. "How disappointing! I was sure you'd recognize me, Señor Morales. Your paper has mentioned me more than once."

"Too many times," his partner rumbled.

"Pedro, who is this man?" Gallardo asked.

"I don't know and I don't care. But he'd better get out of here right now before I call the police!"

"Easy, Pedro," the publisher cautioned. "Don't provoke them."

Fernandez edged away from the editor's vicinity.

"You won't call the police," the small man said.

"You think not? Just watch me!" Morales reached for the phone on his desk.

The small man fired once, from the hip. The gunshot wasn't as loud as the sound of the telephone being blown apart.

Fernandez cried out and cowered in the corner. Gallardo was white-faced and shaken.

Morales touched his face. It was streaked with small cuts inflicted by plastic shards from the phone.

"You—you've made your point," Morales said weakly. "Now, who are you and what do you want?"

"You're a cool one," the small man said admiringly.

"We'll make it hot for him, eh?" his partner said with a chuckle.

Gallardo reached into his pants pocket. The gun muzzle swiveled to cover him.

"I'm getting my wallet," the publisher said. "Take the money but don't hurt anyone."

"We're not robbers!" the muscleman said indignantly.

"Then who are you?"

"Allow me to introduce myself. I am Garcia Espinosa." The small man's oversize head inclined in a mocking bow. "And this is my dear friend, Ugarte."

The big man grinned.

"Espinosa!" Fernandez gasped.

"Ah, you *have* heard of me. That is so gratifying."

"Who is he, Pedro?" Gallardo hissed.

Now Morales was afraid. "A hoodlum. Racketeer—arsonist—killer."

"What does he want with us?!" Fernandez croaked.

"A simple answer," Espinosa said. "The identity of your source. But we eavesdropped outside long enough to know you don't have it."

"Too bad," Ugarte said.

Espinosa took a photo off the desk. "It's very thoughtful of you to arrange all the material for us."

"Is that what all this is about?" Gallardo demanded. "The plane crash?"

"*Sí.*"

"You were the one on the phone who told me to drop the investigation," Morales said.

"You should have heeded my warning," Espinosa said.

"You want the story killed?" Gallardo asked. "Fine, it's done. We won't have anything more to do with it."

"For God's sake, Julio, show some integrity!" Morales snapped.

Gallardo sighed. "All the information is right there on the desk. Take it. I promise we won't print another word on the subject. I swear it."

"Julio, don't—" Morales began.

"Shut up, you fool!" Gallardo was red-faced and shouting. "I'm trying to keep us alive!"

"Save your breath," Morales said. "Look at them! You think they're going to let us live?"

"Why not? We'll make a deal. That's how business is done. This won't be the first story we've killed because somebody didn't like it. What about it, Espinosa? You'll deal, won't you?"

"Perhaps," Espinosa said. "You have other copies of these documents?"

"No," Gallardo said. "I don't think so. You didn't make any copies of this stuff, did you, Pedro?"

Morales shook his head. "You poor fool."

"Answer me, Morales! I demand to know if there are any more copies!"

"Yes!" Morales said. "Yes, there are copies! And if anything happens to me, they'll be sent to the proper authorities!"

"Are you out of your mind?" Gallardo shouted. "You can't bluff these men! You said yourself that they're killers!"

"I'm not bluffing," Morales said quietly.

"I think you are," Espinosa said. "You're not very cooperative, Señor Morales. Perhaps your assistant will be more forthcoming. Make him talk, Ugarte."

Ugarte moved toward Fernandez.

"No! No!" Fernandez was trapped in a corner. He waved his hands in front of his face, as if that would ward off Ugarte.

"He's lying! There are no copies!"

"You know what you've done, Fernandez? You've killed us all," Morales said.

"No! Oh, no!" Fernandez covered his face with his hands.

"Why all this talk of killing?" Espinosa asked. "You're a morbid man, Morales. Didn't you hear what Señor Gallardo said? This is just a business deal."

"That's right," Gallardo eagerly agreed. "Everybody knows you don't kill a newspaperman. There are two kinds of people you don't kill: policemen and newspapermen."

"Sure, everybody knows that." Espinosa tossed his briefcase to Ugarte. "Get the ropes."

Ugarte took some short lengths of rope out of the briefcase. They looked like bits of string in his huge hands.

"What are those for?" Gallardo asked suspiciously.

"To ensure that you stay put while we make our getaway," Espinosa said.

Morales tried to make a break. He jumped up, overturning his chair.

Espinosa moved to cover him. Morales charged Espinosa and his gun.

Ugarte grabbed Morales by the neck with both hands and lifted him up off the floor.

Espinosa covered Fernandez and Gallardo, but he needn't have bothered. They were frozen in place, horror-struck.

Ugarte held Morales at arm's length to avoid his kicking feet. Eyes bulged and the tongue stuck out of the editor's purpling face.

"What do I do with him?" Ugarte showed no sign of strain at holding a 185-pound man in the air.

Ugarte carried Morales across the room and dashed the back of his head against the wall.

"No!" Fernandez shrieked.

The wall plaster cracked at the point of impact. Ugarte slammed Morales's head against it again. The sound of the blow didn't hide the dry snap of Morales's neck breaking.

"No! Oh, my God, no!" Fernandez cried.

"Shhhh," Espinosa said. "Or Ugarte will have to silence you, too."

Ugarte let go of the body. Morales slid down the wall, the back of his head marking it with a bright crimson smear. He sat down hard, toppled, then lay stretched on the floor with his head twisted at an unnatural angle.

"You're insane!" Gallardo rasped. "He was right! You are going to kill us!"

"Calm yourself, señor. After all, it's only business," Espinosa said. "Besides, if I were going to kill you, I wouldn't bother to have you tied up, would I? Tie them up, Ugarte.''

Ugarte stood motionless, his eyes vacant as he stared down at Morales.

"Ugarte! Do what I told you!"

Ugarte snapped out of it. A sneer replaced his blank expression. "He was stupid."

"No, no! He was a brave man," Espinosa protested. "But what good is courage when you don't have the guns to back it up? No good at all."

Espinosa smoked a cigarette while Ugarte herded Gallardo and Fernandez together behind the desk. Gallardo couldn't stop shaking. Fernandez was near catatonia.

Ugarte stretched them out on the floor and tied them hand and foot. "Better gag them too," Espinosa said.

"Do I have to?"

"Please. They've already made enough noise. We're lucky we're up so high that nobody on the street can hear them."

"Then why bother to gag them?"

"Because I don't want to hear them," Espinosa said. "I have sensitive ears."

"But—"

"Just do it! It's neater that way."

"All right," Ugarte grumbled. "You're the boss."

"Wait a minute," Gallardo said. "Stop and think what you're doing. I'm a wealthy man. I can pay you. I have plenty of money—"

"You keep it," Ugarte said. When he finished gagging both men, he fished Gallardo's wallet out of the publisher's pocket.

"I lied when I said we weren't robbers. But it's not our main line of work." Ugarte took the money out of the wallet. "Hmmmm, not much here . . ."

"Rich men don't need cash," Espinosa snorted. "They've got credit cards."

"What now?"

"Get the juice."

Ugarte exited the office. The big man was light on his feet and moved almost soundlessly.

Espinosa lit a fresh cigarette and smoked it while sitting on the windowsill. Despite the lateness of the hour, a fair amount of traffic cruised the streets. None of the pedestrians who passed the newspaper building gave it a second look.

Espinosa didn't hear Ugarte's footsteps, but he knew the big man was returning when he heard sloshing sounds in the hall.

Ugarte carried four plastic jugs filled with a mixture of gasoline, oil, and water. The mixture burned more efficiently than plain gasoline.

When they smelled the gasoline, Gallardo and Fernandez cried out through their gagged mouths.

"Put one jug under the desk and one next to the filing cabinet," Espinosa said. "Spread the other two around."

When the two jugs were in place, Ugarte opened the third and poured it on the desk.

"Use plenty. We want to burn up all the documents," Espinosa said. "Careful—don't get any on yourself."

"I won't. Should I baptise our friends?"

"By all means."

Ugarte uncapped the fourth jug and wetted down the captives, then worked his way around the desk toward the door. Tossing aside the empty jug, he said, "That's that."

Espinosa nodded. "That should do it."

"Can I light the fire?"

"Of course you can." Espinosa's smile was fondly indulgent.

They stepped outside the office. Ugarte lit a match. "Now?"

"Now."

Holding the matchbook by the corner of its cover, Ugarte set fire to it. His eyes were dreamy again.

Fernandez was in shock and didn't react. Gallardo wriggled across the floor toward the open door.

"Adiós, amigos!" Espinosa said.

Ugarte tossed the flaming matchbook into the office. It bounded across the carpet and came to rest in the middle of the floor.

The volatile mixture ignited with a *whoosh*, filling the room with flames.

Firelight illuminated the vast, dim city room. Ugarte and Espinosa ran to the stairs.

The fire touched off the two full jugs. They exploded like napalm bombs, unleashing a hellish fire storm.

A corpse sprawled on the landing—the night watchman whom Ugarte had killed earlier. The big man and Espinosa stepped over the body and ran down the stairs.

They exited the building by a side door and were a city block away before the first excited spectators came on the scene.

They savored their handiwork from a safe distance, loving the crowd, the clamor, and the spectacle of the inferno.

"Pretty sight, isn't it?" Espinosa noticed that Ugarte was pouting. "Why the long face, my friend?"

"Too bad we had to gag them. It's better when you can hear them scream."

"Cheer up! There'll be others."

THREE

APUCHAKA IN CRITICAL, POSSIBLY TERMINAL PHASE. LABOR FORCE INFILTRATED BY SOVIET AND CUBAN AGENTS. PROJECT ALSO THREATENED BY INTERNAL CORRUPTION. HAVE EVIDENCE OF CONSPIRACY INPLICATING HIGHEST ADMINISTRATIVE LEVELS. WILL SUPPLY DETAILS SOONEST.

MANDRAKE

"Mandrake was Colonel Dunninger's code name," Hawk said. "That's the text of the last message he sent before he disappeared."

Nick Carter put the transcription back on his chief's desk. "A conspiracy at the highest levels—that's a provocative statement."

"I think so. And I'm glad you share my opinion, Nick, because this is your next assignment."

White-haired, fierce-eyed David Hawk was the director of AXE, the ultrasecret intelligence organization. Nick Carter was his premier agent.

The briefing was being held in Hawk's inner sanctum in AXE headquarters, located on Dupont Circle in Washington, D.C.

"Dunninger's heyday was a bit before your time, Nick. He was a key player in the CIA's covert action team during Ike's administration."

"I'm familiar with the man's record, sir," Carter said. "It was outstanding."

"Dunninger was one of the best." Hawk's gaze softened as he thought back. "He and his sidekick, Buzz Kelly, were right in the thick of some of the biggest coups of the era: Guatemala in '54, the Magsaysay election in the Philippines, the Congo in the early '60s . . ."

"But he was forced out of the CIA, wasn't he?"

"Oh, yes." Hawk's voice hardened. "Dunninger went on record with his protest that the planned invasion of Cuba was doomed to fail. That didn't sit well with the top brass. Before they could exile him to bureaucratic limbo, he handed in his resignation."

"Too bad they ignored his prediction."

Hawk nodded. "After the Bay of Pigs fiasco, Dunninger was one of the few spooks to retain any credibility with Kennedy. He went to work for the White House as a global Troubleshooter."

Hawk paused to take a cigar from his desktop humidor, lit it, then continued. "The Apuchaka project was Dunninger's Waterloo."

Hawk rolled the cigar in his fingers, its foul smoke floating in the air around him.

"The project was a joint venture of the U.S. and the South American Alliance for Progress, an economic development plan designed to counter Castro-style insurgency. It ran into trouble from the start. The more millions that were poured down the hole, the slower the work progressed. President Johnson sent Dunninger to Peru to investigate."

Hawk tapped some ash from the end of his cigar. "Dunninger sent his last message and hired a private plane to fly him to Lima. The plane disappeared somewhere in the mountains."

"And the project?" Carter asked.

"Once again, Dunninger was right. The project was terminal. Two days after he vanished, the Apuchaka railway bridge was blown up by Communist guerrillas. That scuttled the project. Its failure helped prompt the military junta to take control of the country."

"And there the story ended," Carter said, "until now."

"The files were closed on the case. The White House was preoccupied with the Vietnam mess. The CIA didn't think the matter was worth looking into. Which was a pity, since they were running a lot of agents in Peru at the time, agents who have since risen to prominence in the ranks of the Company."

Carter leaned forward. "You think some of them were recruited by the opposition?"

"That's what you're going to find out," Hawk said.

"Twenty years makes for a cold trail, sir."

"It's not cold anymore," Hawk said. "It's red-hot."

Hawk stuck the cigar between his lips. It had gone out. Carter reached across the desk with his lighter. The cigar caught fire.

"Thanks," Hawk said gruffly. He leaned back in his chair and puffed acrid smoke.

"If the Soviets did manage to turn some CIA operatives in Peru, then they've had their moles in the Company for over two decades. You can imagine how they'll fight to protect those assets. That's why I'm assigning a Killmaster to the case."

Hawk used the cigar as a pointer to emphasize his remarks. "That's why I'm sending you."

FOUR

Carter disembarked from the AeroPeru jet at Lima's Jorge Chavez airport.

The terminal building was vast, dim, and gloomy. Security was provided by a large number of uniformed policemen armed with machine pistols.

The customs line was slow-moving. A smartly dressed woman three places ahead of Carter was perspiring, white-faced and stiff with anxiety. He wondered what the amateur was smuggling. Most likely it was jewelry or currency. Drugs were smuggled *out* of Peru, not into it.

A customs official signaled to two of his subordinates. They removed the protesting woman from the line and escorted her to a back room to be strip-searched by a matron.

The rest of the travelers buzzed with nervous whispers.

Then it was Carter's turn to come under scrutiny. His examiner was a soft-faced man with hard eyes. He gave Carter's bags a thorough going-over and carefully compared the American's face to the passport photo.

The passport was issued to George Markham. The identity was fake but the passport was authentic, courtesy of AXE's technical support division.

"The purpose of your visit, Señor Markham?" the examiner asked.

"Business," Carter said.

"How long will you be staying?"

"Not long. I should have things wrapped up in a few weeks."

The examiner returned Carter's passport. "Enjoy your visit to Peru, señor."

"Thank you."

Carter carried his overnight bag and suitcase to a row of pay telephones. A big clock on the wall gave the time as a few minutes past one in the afternoon.

He stepped into a phone booth, taking his luggage with him. The thieves who preyed on tourists were incredibly quick and could make a suitcase disappear in the blink of an eye.

He dialed the memorized number of a shop in downtown Lima. The call was answered on the third ring.

A man's voice said, "*Antiguedades*."

Carter replied in fluent Spanish. "This is Anthony Blasco from the Gulf Coast. I'd like to make an appointment to view your collection at four this afternoon."

"One moment please, Señor Blasco."

After a pause, a woman came on the line. "Señor Blasco? I'm sorry, but we can't accommodate you at four. May we schedule your appointment for an hour later, at five?"

"Certainly," Carter said. "Five will be fine."

"Very good. Five it is, then. I look forward to making your acquaintance, señor."

"No more than I anticipate the pleasure of meeting you, señorita."

Next, Carter called his hotel to confirm George Markham's reservation.

A horde of taxis jostled for position in front of the terminal. Carter grabbed a cab, settled on the price of the fare in advance, and leaned back in his seat as the taxi took off.

It was an overcast spring day in October, since the seasons were reversed below the equator. The fast-paced anarchy of Peruvian highway driving kept Carter on the edge of his seat during the trip into the city.

Lima was as he remembered it, noisy, dirty, and crowded, but with a rough and rowdy charm.

Carter had the taxi stop a few blocks away from the shopping district of Plaza San Martin. The driver's attempt at boosting the fare above the agreed-upon price came to a halt when he took a good look at Carter's grim face. He drove away in a hurry.

Bags in hand, Carter entered the plaza. Going from store to store, he purchased a man's wig, a sports jacket several sizes too large for him, a pair of baggy gray trousers, and a pair of inexpensive loafers.

The Hotel Marsano was located a few blocks north of the Plaza San Martin and a few blocks south of the Plaza de Armas in the center of the city. Carter's room was on the third floor at the rear of the building.

Carter stripped to his underwear and put on the clothes he'd bought on his shopping trip. He modeled the wig in front of the bathroom mirror. Some trimming with a scissors made it look slightly more convincing.

He put on a pair of wire-rimmed glasses whose lenses were clear glass. He tried on a variety of expressions until he found one that suited his characterization of Anthony Blasco, an older and wearier gentleman.

He adjusted his posture and carriage to fit the role. Hunching forward subtracted inches from his height. His expression was mild and preoccupied.

Characterization, not cosmetics, was the key to a successful disguise. Anthony Blasco would undergo only casual scrutiny that would not require an extensive makeover.

A battered soft felt hat concealed most of the wig.

Without his weapons, Carter was only half dressed. He set out to remedy that lack.

Carter stepped out into the empty hall. He fastened a hair-fine strip of clear plastic adhesive across the door and its frame, a foot above the floor. The simple warning device would tell him if his room had been entered during his absence.

He took the stairs to the second floor, then rode the elevator to the lobby and exited via the front entrance. Not even the doorman gave him a second glance.

He followed the broad thoroughfare of the Jiron de la Union south back to the Plaza San Martin. He crossed the plaza, going east on the fashionable, expensive avenue of the Colmena.

The glittering avenue held high-priced hotels, fancy restaurants, and exclusive shops. He strolled past a store whose display window exhibited pre-Columbian artifacts. Gilt letting spelled out its name: ANTIGUEDADES.

Carter went to the end of the block, crossed the street, and walked back in the opposite direction. He detected no sign that the shop was under surveillance, which didn't necessarily mean that it wasn't.

A half hour remained before his four o'clock appointment. The business about a five o'clock appointment was part of a recognition code to establish his bona fides.

The antique shop was AXE's Lima station.

Carter killed time by having a cool drink at a sidewalk café. He enjoyed the parade of beautiful women passing by, but they were oblivious to the existence of non-descript Anthony Blasco.

Four o'clock found Carter pressing the doorbell of the antique store.

A stocky, dark-haired young man with a mustache looked at him through the grillwork covering the glass door. He spoke through the intercom:

"May I help you, please?"

"Anthony Blasco. I have a five o'clock appointment."

"It's only four o'clock now."

"*Si.*"

The door was unlocked and opened. "Please come in, Señor Blasco.

"*Gracias.*"

The long, narrow shop resembled a museum of Incan artifacts. The beige walls were hung with pieces of centuries-old woven fabric. Intricate silver and gold jewelry was displayed in glass cases. Ceramic vessels from several pre-Columbian Peruvian civilizations stood on pedestals on either side of the ribbon of rainbow-colored rug that ran down the center aisle.

"How do you do, señor? I am Alfonso Villafirmo," the young man said.

Carter shook his hand. "Pleased to meet you."

"Señora Rinaldi is expecting you. This way, please."

Carter followed him to the rear of the display area, where a thirtyish blond-haired man with tortoiseshell glasses sat behind a massive antique desk.

Villafirmo introduced him. "Señor Blasco, meet my associate, Peter Cates."

"We can dispense with the tradecraft," Cates said, extending his hand. "Welcome aboard, Mr. Carter."

Carter shook his hand, but said with a straight face,

"You've mistaken me for someone else. I'm Anthony Blasco."

"Come on, Carter," Cates groaned. "You can drop the cloak-and-dagger stuff now. You're among friends."

"My friends know enough not to break cover," Carter said in his natural voice.

"Are you kidding?" Cates was incredulous. "You think the place is bugged? I assure you it's not."

"If a lipreader is watching us with binoculars, you've just blown my cover." Carter's back was turned to the shop's front windows.

Cates didn't know whether to be amused or angry. He shook his head in disbelief. "You guys in the field are just too paranoid."

"There's no such thing as being too paranoid," Carter told him. "Not in this game."

"Yeah, you're right. Celia's waiting for you." Cates activated his desk-top intercom: "Mr. Blasco's here to see you."

"Send him in," came the reply.

Cates gestured at the door behind his desk. "Straight through there, Mr. Blasco."

A buzzer electronically unlocked the door, which was solid metal covered with a thin wooden veneer.

A few paces beyond it lay a second door, which opened at his approach.

Carter entered a square-shaped, windowless room, filled with filing cabinets with combination locks and banks of sophisticated electronic equipment.

Celia Rinaldi was the chief of AXE's Lima station. It was a small outpost, but so was AXE: compactness ensured efficiency, security, and secrecy.

She was a honey-haired blonde with jade-green eyes

and bronze skin. She wore a lightweight cream-colored jacket and skirt combination and a gray blouse. Not even the conservative cut of her outfit could camouflage her voluptuous hourglass figure.

Her welcoming smile ripened into laughter. "Oh, Nick, what a sight you are!"

"You're a sight for sore eyes, Celia."

She stood up and came to greet him. Carter wrapped his arms around her and pressed her to him. He tilted her head up toward his lips.

"Please, Nick, not during working hours," she chuckled, deftly easing out of his embrace. "Business before pleasure."

"I was afraid you'd say that," Carter sighed.

"Besides, I feel funny kissing you in that getup." She looked at him appraisingly. "Actually, the disguise is rather effective. It's knowing that you're really Nick Carter that makes it seem a bit outlandish."

She stepped back and took another long look. "Hmmmm . . . the jacket's too large, even for your broad shoulders, Nick."

"I need the extra room for my gun."

"Can't say I'm mad about the material, either."

"Tony Blasco's no fashion plate," Carter said. "And speaking of my gun, I think you have something for me. If you don't, I'm in trouble."

"Not to worry."

Celia handed him a sealed diplomatic pouch. "This got to Peru before you did."

"With airport security being beefed up all over the world, it's getting harder and harder for an honest spy to smuggle weapons across borders," Carter said. "Let's hear it for diplomatic immunity."

"Don't let Ambassador McLarran hear you say that.

He hasn't any use for spooks as it is. If he knew how we were using his diplomatic privileges, he'd hit the ceiling.''

Carter grinned. "He may hit it yet, before I'm through with this job."

He eagerly unsealed the pouch and emptied its contents on Celia's desk: a 9mm Luger holstered in a shoulder rig, a stiletto in a chamois sheath, and a half-dozen walnut-size mini-bombs.

"Ahhh . . ." Carter savored the lifting of the nagging sense of unease that had bothered him ever since he'd been separated from the tools of his trade.

He took off his jacket, rolled up his right shirt sleeve, and fastened the chamois sheath to the inside of his forearm. He rolled the sleeve back down, concealing the blade.

He unholstered the Luger and checked it.

"I wish you could see your face right now," Celia said. "Wilhelmina's your only steady lady, Nick."

"She's my better half, all right." Carter worked the pistol's action, finding everything in order.

He strapped on the shoulder holster, slapped a loaded clip into the Luger, and holstered it. "Now I'm ready for business."

"A nasty business it is, too, with degenerates like these." Celia put some photographs on the desk. "Here are the two stars of your hit parade."

The full-face and profile shots had the stark lighting characteristic of police mug shots.

Carter picked one up. "This guy looks like a comic book caricature of a mad scientist."

"He's mad, all right. That's Garcia Espinosa."

"The man who sets fires, eh?"

"A pyromaniac and a pathological sadist," Celia said. "Also reputed to be a dead shot with a pistol."

"I'll be careful not to let him get the drop on me."

"His partner's another pea from the same pod," Celia said, "Juan Maria Pacifico de la Cruz—alias 'Ugarte.' Being born into one of Peru's finest and oldest families did nothing to hamper his career of crime. The record of his sex crimes reads like something out of Krafft-Ebing. But that's just his way of amusing himself between jobs. His trade is violence. A big hulking brute who likes to kill with his bare hands."

"A fine pair," Carter mused. "Quite an odd couple."

"They met a few years ago in Lurigancho Prison. That's where these photos were taken. That's also where they made their contacts with the radical underground. The prison was a hotbed of revolutionary fanatics and Shining Path rebels."

"They don't strike me as political types," Carter said, "but then, neither were the Mafiosi who did jobs for the Red Brigades in Italy a few years ago."

"Ugarte and Espinosa's only allegiance is to money —and each other. Lately they've done a lot of work for Soviet-backed Marxist factions, but they'll hire out to anybody who can pay their fee."

"And that's where I come in," Carter said. "Or, rather, that's where George Markham enters the picture."

"Correct. How does it feel to be a man of property?"

"I'll let you know when I've seen the property," Carter said.

"Oh, it's a prime piece of real estate, all right," Celia said with a smile. "A Callao warehouse that's an eyesore and a rattrap."

"Good. Nobody will miss it if it burns down. I'd like to get a look at it today."

"Alfonso will tell you how to get there. He bought

the property for George Markham.''

"Good. He seems to know what he's doing," Carter said. "If I need to call on you for any backup, I'd prefer it if you used him, not Cates."

"Any reason why?" Celia's tone implied that she already knew the answer.

"I don't like Cates's attitude."

"Peter is quite brilliant at analyzing and forecasting economic trends, but he doesn't have the temperament for clandestine operations."

"I'll say."

"He just doesn't understand how easily people kill each other in the name of ideology."

"That could be a fatal naïveté," Carter said.

"I've recommended that he be recalled to Washington. He belongs behind a desk at headquarters. But in the meantime, I have to make do with the personnel I've got. I'm so glad you're here, Nick."

"You can express your gratitude by letting me take you out tonight for dinner and drinks and who-knows-what-else."

"Sorry, darling, but you're already booked up this evening."

"Who's the lucky lady?" Carter asked.

"Xica Bandeira is her name and she's no lady," Celia said. "But with any luck, she's your pipeline to Ugarte and Espinosa—and beyond them, to the mystery man who runs the Marxist murder network in Peru."

"Should be an interesting night," Carter said.

FIVE

Callao is the port city of landlocked Lima. The warehouse was located in a run-down quarter of the waterfront district. Carter had to sweeten the fare with an extra cash bonus to convince the cabdriver to take him there.

The cab pulled up in front of the building a few hours before sundown.

Carter gave the driver some more money. "Wait for me and I'll make it worth your while."

"Don't be too long, señor. It's not safe here after dark. For that matter, it's not safe before dark."

The long, hangarlike warehouse sat on a pier, facing its narrow side to the street. A chain link fence topped with barbed wire surrounded it. A rotting, swaybacked dock was its neighbor on the left; on the right stood a crumbling cannery that had gone out of business fifteen years earlier.

A padlocked chain secured the main gate. Carter opened it with a key provided by Celia.

A fat, dull-eyed watchman waddled out of the guard shack. "Hey, señor! What do you think you are doing?"

"Visiting my property," Carter said.

"Who the hell are you?"

"I'm Markham. Weren't you notified of my arrival?"

"Oh, you are Señor Markham. Yes, of course. How stupid of me. You are the new owner. A thousand pardons, señor."

"Don't you want to see some identification?"

"Yes, I suppose that would be a good idea."

The watchman barely glanced at the Markham passport. Rubiro was his name. He was employed by a private security firm that had been hired by the lawyers who handled the sale of the property.

"I'd like to take a look at my property," Carter said.

"Certainly, señor. I'll be right with you, as soon as I lock up the gate."

"Let my driver get in here first." Carter figured that the taxi would be less likely to take off without him if it were parked inside the fence.

The cab pulled into the yard, parking beside Rubiro's jalopy while the watchman locked up.

Key ring in hand, Rubiro gave Carter the grand tour of the premises.

The site was bare of any company name or logo. It's only identification mark was the number of its street address—535—stenciled on a rusty metal plaque hung over the gate.

Celia proved to be a master of understatement. Not only was the property an eyesore, but it stank, too. The yard and a good part of the pier were heaped high with fifty-gallon drums filled with industrial waste that gave off a noxious chemical reek.

She hadn't been wrong about the rats, either. A horde of them scampered among the drums, chittering at the two-legged intruders.

Rubiro unlocked the door to the main building. Its electric power had been cut off long ago. Weak gray light filtered through the filthy skylights, pushing back the darkness at the center of the space. Beyond it,

Rubiro's flashlight was needed to pick out details.

More toxic waste canisters were stored inside the warehouse. Their smell was stifling and unhealthy. Carter held a handkerchief over his nose and mouth.

For the next half hour, Carter prowled the property. He memorized the layout, mentally fixing the position of entrances and exits, places of concealment, and possible escape routes.

"That's all of it, señor," Rubiro said when the tour was done.

"You've done a fine job here," Carter said.

"Gracias, señor."

"I'm afraid your services won't be required anymore."

"But, señor—"

"Frankly, there doesn't seem to be anything here worth protecting," Carter said. "But I appreciate your good work, and I want you to have this two weeks' severance pay."

"Muchas gracias, señor!" Rubiro made the money vanish.

"Please notify your company that I won't be needing any guards in the future."

"Certainly, señor."

"In fact, there's no reason why you can't go off duty right now. I'll lock up."

Rubiro turned the key ring over to Carter, started his car, and drove away.

After locking up, Carter told the cabdriver to take him back to Lima.

The driver asked cautiously, "That property belongs to you, señor?"

"Yes."

The driver shook his head. "What a pity."

SIX

They called themselves "Los Hidalgos," taking their name from the impoverished knights who left Spain to carve out an empire for themselves in the New World. They were a violently embittered clique of university students whose wealthy families' property had been expropriated by the junta for redistribution to the peasants. They were hotheaded reactionaries seething with resentment.

Four of them lurked behind the bushes of the campus grounds at twilight.

Martin Santiago was the driving force of the team. He was considerably older than the others, closer in age to the instructors than to his fellow students. He was slight, bony, bearded, and wild eyed.

"Here he comes!" he hissed.

An older gentleman carrying a bookbag tucked under his arm ambled along the curving path that stretched between the university buildings.

"Be sure to cover your faces," Santiago said.

Following his example, the others tied dark scarves over the lower halves of their faces. They all wore dark clothes.

"Some others are coming," one of the young men whispered.

"We'll be done before they get here," Santiago said.

"If they interfere, so much the worse for them," another added.

"We just want the professor," Santiago said. "Shh! He's almost here."

Professor Oswaldo Jaramillo had just finished teaching a night course in economics for graduate students. The mildly left-leaning academic was known for his thesis that the communal basis of Inca society could provide a model for improving the lot of their descendants, the subsistence-level *campesinos*.

This hardly revolutionary theory had nonetheless targeted him for punishment by the Hidalgos. Martin Santiago had called him to their attention.

The professor drew abreast of the shrubbery where the extremists lurked.

One of them whispered, "Now?"

"Now!" Santiago said.

They burst out of the bushes and surrounded the professor.

"What—what do you want?" Jaramillo gasped.

"We want Marxist scum like you out of the university!" Santiago said.

"You've poured enough poison into students' ears," another accused.

Jaramillo was frightened but he wouldn't crawl. "You're mad, all of you! Get out of my way!"

"Let's teach the teacher a lesson, brothers!" Santiago said.

A violent shove from behind sent the professor sprawling. He dropped his bag, spilling books on the path.

The Hidalgos ringed him, knocking him this way and

that. A vicious slap broke his glasses in two. He raised his hands to protect his face.

Santiago slammed a brutal punch into the professor's belly, doubling him over.

Fists pummeled Jaramillo. He buckled at the knees, but his tormentors wouldn't let him fall. They held him so they could continue beating him.

"Hit him some more!"

"Look, he's fainted, the weakling."

Some students at the top of the path saw what was happening. One of them began to shout.

Another ran to get help.

"Enough!" Santiago commanded. "We won't kill him. Not this time."

They let go of Jaramillo, who fell hard to the pavement. Ribs cracked from one last brutal kick.

"I said, let's go!" Santiago ordered.

The four men darted behind the bushes and took off at a run. Their escape route took them through a dimly lit grove of trees and across a vacant lot.

"Stop!" Santiago said. "Take off your scarves. Put them away."

The others obeyed.

"Don't run. Walk as if you hadn't a care in the world," Santiago said.

He ducked under low-hanging branches and led them down a dirt path to a parking lot at the rear of a dormitory.

The getaway car sat waiting. It had been stolen for this job. It was rigged with license plates stolen from a second car as an added precaution.

"How did it go?" the driver asked excitedly. "Did you get the dirty bastard? I wish I'd been with you—"

Santiago reached through the open window and

slapped the driver. "Idiot! I told you to leave the motor running!"

"I—I'm sorry!"

"You'll be a lot sorrier if the engine doesn't start."

The Hidalgos piled into the car, attracting mildly curious glances from a handful of students loafing on the back steps. The idlers were too far away to see any faces clearly.

Santiago sat in the front seat. The driver hit the ignition and tromped on the gas pedal.

"Don't flood it," Santiago cautioned. "And drive slowly! Don't attract attention."

The driver heaved a sigh of relief as the engine turned over and the car started. He eased out of the parking lot into the street.

Santiago reminded him to turn on the lights. "And slow down, slow down! We got away clean. The only way we can get caught is if we're stopped for speeding."

"Nobody's following," reported a fellow in the back seat.

Santiago permitted himself a thin smile of satisfaction. "You see? That's how easily it's done."

He told the driver when to make right and left turns. The car wove a circuitous route through the city until Santiago was positive they hadn't been tailed.

"A fine night's work, brothers," he said at last. "That'll show the Reds that we're not going to sit back and let them take over the country!"

"Let's go out and celebrate," somebody suggested. "We'll make a night of it."

"No, my brothers. We have cause for celebration, but not tonight. We won't call attention to ourselves. We'll separate and spend the rest of the night quietly at our own homes. When we meet again in a few days—

after the hue and cry subsides—we'll have a proper celebration. And," he added, "we'll plan our next operation."

One by one the Hidalgos were dropped off on various street corners until only Santiago and the driver remained.

"Pull over," Santiago told him. "You can get out here. I'll get rid of the car."

"Thanks. Many thanks, brother! I—I hope I did all right."

"You did your job." Santiago squeezed the driver's shoulder. "Next time, you'll do better."

"I must admit, I was scared when I was waiting for you all to return."

"It's natural. You'll get over it after a few more jobs," Santiago said.

The driver said good night and got out. Santiago got behind the wheel and drove away.

He parked on a dark side street a few blocks east of Avenida Abancay. He used his scarf to wipe down the car, removing telltale fingerprints.

He left the keys in the ignition, having no doubt that the car would be stolen in a matter of minutes, further muddying his tracks.

A quarter hour later found him at a bus stop not far from the Parque Universitario, the bustling hub of the city's mass transit system.

A dozen people clustered at the stop. The bench was full. One of its occupants was a portly, middle-aged bearded man reading a newspaper.

He glanced up as Santiago passed him, then returned his gaze to his paper.

Had he folded his paper and put it under his arm, he would have signaled Santiago that he was under surveillance and warned him away.

Santiago was cautious. The lack of a warning signal meant only that his contact had failed to detect any watchers. Santiago had to satisfy himself that all was well.

He went to the end of the street, crossed it, then worked his way back until he was opposite the bus stop. He detected nothing out of the ordinary.

Ten minutes more, and a bus halted at the stop. When it departed, the bearded man sat alone on the bench.

Santiago crossed the street and sat down beside him. The duo exchanged no sign of recognition.

"How did it go?" the bearded man asked.

"No problem."

They whispered out of the corners of their mouths, jailhouse style.

"And Professor Jaramillo?"

"Tomorrow you'll read in the paper that the professor was set upon by a gang of rightist thugs," Santiago said.

The bearded man chuckled. "The Hidalgos are useful idiots. How considerate of them to do our work for us and take all the blame. You didn't let them go too far?"

"Just far enough."

"Good. Dead, he's a martyr. Crippled, he's a living reminder that neutrality cannot be tolerated in the struggle to establish the dictatorship of the proletariat."

They fell silent as a pair of young lovers strolled by, arm in arm. When the couple had passed out of earshot, Santiago asked, "Anything else on the agenda?"

"Not right now."

"What about the Apuchaka affair?"

"It's stabilized, so far," the bearded man replied. "I detect signs of motion on the part of our enemies, but there's nothing definite yet."

"Any leads on who tipped off *La República*?"

"They haven't shown their hand yet, whoever they are."

"When they do—" Santiago began.

"When they do, I'll give friend Espinosa a call," the bearded man finished.

"I don't trust him. He's everything the revolution opposes. What's more, he's crazy in the head."

"Crazy like a fox, you mean. Espinosa's a tool, like the Hidalgos. They do the dirty work so we can keep our hands clean."

"When Espinosa's outlived his usefulness, let me be the one to finish him off," Santiago requested.

"That may not be for some time."

"But when the time comes . . ."

"He's yours," the bearded man promised.

"I'm looking forward to it," Santiago said.

A few hours later, the bearded man approached the reception desk of a hospital not far from the University of San Marcos.

His face set in an expression of grave concern, he said, "Excuse me, please."

The nurse-receptionist looked up from a form she was filling out.

"I heard the terrible news about Professor Jaramillo," the bearded man said. "I understand he was brought here for treatment."

"Yes, he was. It's shocking! What kind of animals would do a thing like that?"

"Terrible, just terrible. And how is the professor?"

"He was just operated on. He's in the recovery room."

"How—how serious were his injuries?"

"His condition is critical."

The bearded man seemed ready to burst into tears.

Two surgeons in green scrub suits crossed the hall.

The nurse said, "There's Dr. Bustos, who did the operation. He can tell you about the patient's condition better than I."

"Muchas gracias."

The bearded man hurried after the surgeons. "Dr. Bustos! Dr. Bustos!"

"I'm Bustos," the older of the pair said.

"Pardon me, Doctor. Professor Jaramillo is a dear friend of mind. Is he—is he going to make it?"

Bustos took a deep breath. "The patient sustained serious damage. The broken bones aren't as life-threatening as his internal injuries. His advanced age is another complicating factor. Still, his condition has stabilized and his vital signs are strong."

"He's got a tremendous will to live," the other surgeon said.

"There are no guarantees, but at this point I'd say there's a good chance he'll pull through," Bustos concluded.

"Thank God for that!" the bearded man said.

The surgeons, impatient to be elsewhere, went on their way.

The bearded man entered a combination gift and flower shop adjacent to the reception area.

He went directly to the book display. Poetry is very popular in Peru, and the store stocked an extensive selection. The bearded man scanned the rack and grunted with satisfaction at finding a certain slim volume of verse.

He showed it to the sales clerk. "See this? *Sunrise at*

Galápagos, by Leon Corona."

The clerk glanced at him with indifferent eyes. "Would you like to purchase it, señor?"

"Purchase it? I wrote it. I am Leon Corona!"

"Oh. Oh! That's nice. I'm sure it's wonderful." She returned to reading a paperback romance.

"Why don't I autograph a few copies?" Corona offered.

"You'd better not."

"Why? It increases the value. A first edition, signed by the author. A collector's item!"

"The book can't be returned if there's an inscription inside it, señor."

Corona was incredulous. "Who would want to return it?"

"I mean, we couldn't return it to the publisher that way."

"Bah!"

Corona put the book back in a prominent position on the shelf. "A question, please."

"Yes?"

"Can a patient receive flowers in intensive care?"

"No, señor."

"That's too bad. Oh, well, I'll send them along when he's feeling better."

The clerk didn't bother to reply. She didn't look up as Corono exited.

SEVEN

Carter caught Xica Bandeira's second and last show at the Starlight Room of the Vista del Mar nightclub in the exclusive oceanfront suburb of Miraflores.

A heavy tip to the maître d' got Carter a table at ringside. Elegantly attired in formal evening wear, he attracted more than a few interested glances from female patrons. He ordered a double brandy and settled in to watch the show.

The slickly produced revue was a Las Vegas-influenced version of Latino cabaret. Variety acts alternated with splashy dance numbers featuring a chorus line of long-legged beauties. The house band played disco with a Peruvian flavor.

The beaming master of ceremonies finally announced, "And now, for your entertainment pleasure—the sensational Xica!"

Her name harvested a big round of applause from the crowd.

The stage blacked out. A spotlight picked up a long, sleek leg emerging from behind a curtain at the wings.

The other leg followed and Xica stepped into view. A drum roll accompanied her as she slithered to center stage.

The lights came up, exposing Xica in all her glory.

She was a Latin beauty, exotic and provocative. A

tangled mane of auburn hair reached down to the top of her ripely curved derriere. Dark eyes flashed in a high-cheekboned face. Her full-lipped mouth pouted with sullen sensuality. Her high-breasted, long-legged dancer's body was sheathed in a glittering green-sequined gown. Her dress's plunging neckline and slit sides revealed plenty of sleek honey-toned skin.

A musical fanfare erupted and she started to sing.

Carter took a long swallow of his drink.

Xica's thin, husky voice was heavily miked. She sighed and pouted her way through a rendition of that old hit, "Besame Mucho," then mangled a couple of other standards.

She couldn't carry a tune in a wheelbarrow, but it didn't matter because she sold a song with her whole body. Swaying, strutting, and flaunting her fabulous figure, she made love to the microphone and to every man in the audience.

The crowd of well-heeled tourists ate it up.

They brought her back for an encore, an uptempo dance number that really allowed her to show her stuff.

She surely raised the room temperature a few degrees, Carter mused.

After she took her last bow and disappeared in the wings, Carter went backstage.

A stocky character with a face like a bulldog barred the way. A fistful of bills persuaded him to let Carter pass.

The backstage area was crowded with performers, stage crew, sugar daddies and stage-door Johnnies. Showgirls in their spangled finery were birds of paradise.

Carter asked a platinum-haired black Amazon where he could find Xica.

"Won't I do?" she purred.

"You certainly would if I didn't already have a date."

"I'd cost you a lot less than that Brazilian gold-digger." Her sensuous gaze surveyed Carter from head to toe and liked what it saw. "A handsome man like you wouldn't have to buy me anything more than dinner and a few drinks."

"I'd love to, some other time."

The black chorine shrugged. "Suit yourself. Xica's dressing room is at the end of the hallway, to the left."

"Thanks so much," Carter said.

"You'd better have a big bankroll, *hombre*," she called after him. "Xica's expensive!"

How right you are, Carter thought. AXE was paying some real money for Xica's services.

Carter rapped on her dressing room door.

"Who's there?"

"Markham."

"It's not locked," she said.

The cramped dressing room was fragrant with perfumes, powders, lotions, and creams. Wrapped in a white terry robe, Xica sat facing the wall mirror as she removed her makeup.

She glanced at Carter's reflection, got interested, and looked him over in the flesh.

"So you're Markham. You're different from what I expected."

"What did you expect?"

"An older man, heavier and grayer."

"Hope you're not disappointed."

"I won't be," she said lazily, "as long as you've got the money."

She swiveled around on the stool, facing him. "Do

you have it?'' Her voice was a breathy whisper.

Carter withdrew an envelope from his inside jacket pocket and put it in Xica's outstretched hand.

The unsealed envelope contained a hefty chunk of U.S. currency. Xica riffled the bills with the practiced hand of a bank teller.

Dropping the whisper, she accused in a cold, clear voice, ''This is only half the amount I agreed on with Tito.''

''Tito'' was a cover identity adopted by AXE's Alfonso Villafirmo when he made the contact with the singer.

Carter took a second envelope from his jacket. He raised its flap to show her the greenbacks inside, then returned it to his inside breast pocket.

''You'll get the other half after I've met Yavar,'' he said.

''How do I know you won't cheat me?''

''How do I know that Yavar can connect me with Espinosa?'' Carter countered.

Xica's heavy-lidded eyes widened, then narrowed. She slid off the stool and went to the door and peeked outside. Apparently she saw nothing threatening, since she brushed past Carter and sat down.

''Don't be so free with that name,'' she snapped. ''He doesn't like it, and his spies are everywhere.''

''I'm not afraid to play with fire,'' Carter said.

''A very bad joke, señor. Even the *pistoleros* and the big gang lords are afraid to cross . . . that man.''

''Why should I worry? I'm just a businessman with a simple proposition for him.''

''You're either very brave or very stupid, Markham. Or maybe both. Either way, I think you'd better pay me all the money now.''

''I think I'd better call the whole deal off and find

somebody else to set it up.'' Carter reached for the original pay envelope.

Xica moved it out of his grasp. ''Okay. Half now, half later.''

''That's what I like,'' Carter said with a grin. ''A relationship built on mutual trust.''

''I stopped trusting men when I was ten years old.''

''What a fascinating life you must have lived. You'll have to tell me all about it while you get dressed.''

''I must shower first.''

''Be my guest.''

Xica wiped the last of the cold cream off her face. She uncrossed her legs, baring long burnished thighs for an instant, then stood up. Carter was looking at her with undisguised admiration.

''I may just have to slap your face, Markham. You're buying the introduction,'' she said, ''not me.''

''That was my understanding.''

''You're a cool one.'' White teeth gleamed when she smiled. ''I think maybe I could get to like you . . . if you last long enough for me to get to know you.'' Xica moved a folding screen across the rear of the dressing room, blocking Carter's view of the shower stall. ''I don't trust you not to peek.''

She took the envelope with her behind the screen. She shrugged off her robe, but Carter's view of her ended just below the shoulders.

She piled her masses of gleaming hair at the top of her head and wrapped them in a towel, turban style. She turned the taps and the water jetted out of the shower head with a hiss.

The dressing room got hotter and steamier, fogging the wall mirror. Carter smoked two cigarettes before she got out of the shower.

''Need your back toweled?'' he offered.

"No. But you can hand me that dress on top of the bureau."

Xica came out from behind the screen clad in a yellow-and-black print dress. She was braless but her breasts jutted high and firm.

More time passed while she applied fresh makeup and donned her accessories: gold hoop earrings, a necklace made of a dozen delicate gold chains, and a wide gold bracelet.

Standing in front of the mirror, she ran her hands down her flat belly and rounded hips, smoothing her dress.

"Charming," Carter murmured appreciatively.

"I'm hungry. You can buy me dinner, Markham."

"That sounds delightful, but what about Yavar?"

"The night is young. He won't crawl out from under his rock for hours yet."

"Lead on." Carter offered his arm, and she took it.

They went to the Rincon Gaucho restaurant on the Avenida Larco. The eatery specialized in prime cuts of Argentinian beef.

Carter didn't bat an eye when Xica ordered one of the most expensive filets on the menu.

"Sounds good," he told the waiter. "I'll have the same, rare. And your best red wine."

"I'll give you this, Markham: you go first class," Xica said.

"The only way to travel. But don't get the idea that I'm made of money," Carter cautioned.

"All you Americans are fat with dollars."

"I'd like to keep some of them," Carter said.

After wolfing down the main course and the better part of the bottle of wine, she got up from the table.

"No tricks, Xica," Carter warned. "If you're planning on leaving by the back door, remember that I know where to find you.''

"Relax," she said. "I'm just going to powder my nose.''

It was a pretty sure bet that she'd stay the course to collect the rest of her money, but Carter was relieved when she returned a few minutes later.

Xica snuffled and sniffed as if she'd caught a cold. A pair of white smudges frosted her nostrils.

"You weren't kidding about powdering your nose,'' Carter said.

"Eh? What do you mean?''

"Your habit is showing.'' Carter touched his own nose.

Xica rubbed her nose clean with a napkin.

"Now who's playing with fire?'' Carter asked her.

"Don't you worry about me, Markham. I can handle it.''

"I'm not worried about you; I'm worried about me. It's a heavy fall if you get caught with that stuff.''

"Maybe you worry too much. You'd better worry about Yavar.''

"That doesn't worry me a bit,'' Carter said. "That's business.''

"Well, this is my business, so keep your nose out of it . . . unless you want some of the white powder?''

"No, thanks,'' Carter said, lighting a cigarette. "Caffeine is stimulating enough for me.''

Xica was restless during coffee and dessert. "Let's go someplace lively and have a drink.''

"Why not? We're through here, anyhow,'' Carter said.

Carter settled the bill and they started out the front entrance.

A lone man entered.

Xica's grip on Carter's arm tightened. Stress stiffened her face.

The newcomer was a dark, medium-sized man in a gray suit. His wide, pleasant face was partially concealed by tinted aviator glasses and a bushy mustache.

Carter's practiced eye zeroed in on the slight but telltale bulge of a handgun worn high on the man's hip.

The newcomer's face lit up with genuine pleasure. "Xica, darling! How marvelous to see you again!"

"So good to see you, Quintana," Xica said through a tight-lipped smile.

Quintana bowed and kissed her hand.

"Aren't you going to introduce me to the lucky gentleman escorting you, my dear?"

"But of course." Color returned to Xica's face. "George, meet Major Quintana, the famous detective."

"Famous? You are too kind, Xica." Quintana beamed.

"Quintana, this is George Markham," Xica continued, "a visitor from the north."

"How do you do, Major?" Carter stuck out his hand.

Quintana shook it. "Very well, thank you, Señor Markham. You are from the United States? You speak our language excellently."

"You are too kind," Carter echoed Quintana's earlier remark.

"In the interests of accuracy, I should say you speak *my* language excellently. Being Brazilian by birth, Xica's mother tongue is Portuguese. Yes?"

Quintana rubbed his hands together. "So. What brings you so far from your native land, señor?"

"Oh, I'm just looking for a few good investments."

"I wish you luck. Many exciting opportunities await you in Peru—although I daresay none will be as thrilling as the lady who accompanies you this evening."

"A pleasure to make your acquaintance, Major," Carter said, "but I'm afraid we must be going."

"I'm sure we will meet again, señor. And when we do, just call me Quintana. Everybody does."

"And so will I," Carter said, "next time."

"A very good night to you both."

Quintana vanished into the restaurant.

Carter steered her outside. "Cold, Xica? You're trembling."

"It must be a coincidence that he was here tonight. It must be!"

"Sure, he was probably hungry for a good steak dinner. Who's Quintana, Xica? What's his angle?"

"He's a big man in the PIP."

"The Policia de Investigaciónes Peruana?" Carter said. "I've heard they're a lot likc our FBI back home."

"You hear plenty, Markham. Too much. But you've never heard of Quintana, because if you did you'd know he's a very dangerous man."

"More dangerous than, say, Espinosa?"

Xica reflexively looked over her shoulder to make sure no one was listening. But they were alone.

"One's a tarantula and the other's a scorpion," she said.

"Really?" Carter said slowly. "Which is which?"

"They're both poison, *hombre*. And don't ever forget that."

"Let's go for that drink," Carter said. "You look like you could use one."

They took a cab to the center of Lima. They weren't followed, as far as Carter could tell.

Xica wanted to go to a disco, but Carter wasn't in the mood for dancing. They went to the Embassy Club where she downed several pisco sours while he nursed a brandy.

Shortly after midnight and another trip to the rest room to "powder her nose," Xica got restless again.

"The club will be hopping by now, Markham. Let's go."

When she told the cabdriver the destination, he turned around in his seat and stared at her.

"Gato Negro on Avenida Iquitos," she repeated. "You know where that is, don't you?"

"Of course I know where it is," the driver said. "Do you?"

"Don't be rude!"

The driver appealed to Carter. "That's a tough part of town, señor. A man alone can get into a lot of trouble there. They carry them out of the Gato Negro feet-first every night."

"I've got her to protect me," Carter said. "Besides, it sound like a lot of fun."

The ride across town was fun too. Xica snuggled up next to him, her breasts nuzzling his arm. Her breath was warm, too, as she whispered in his ear, "We're almost there. Why not give me the rest of the money?"

"Uh-uh. No Yavar, no money."

She moved away from him to the opposite side of the seat.

The taxi slowed, pulling up alongside a rainbow of garish lights blazing in the middle of a dark and dirty street.

Big, expensive cars lined both sides of the street, many of them guarded by burly, belligerent chauffeurs. A crowd milled on the sidewalks. Overhead, a wild-eyed red neon cat arched its back atop the club marquee. The entrance was flanked by a pair of round windows. Burning in each window was a purple neon sign bearing the club's name: El Gato Negro—the black cat.

A drunk lurched out from between two parked cars and staggered into the side of the cab. He bounced off, sitting down hard in the street, apparently unhurt. The cab speeded up, so his hurled bottle missed it and shattered in the street.

The cab halted at the end of the block to let its passengers out.

Carter paid the fare and tipped the driver.

"It's not too late to change your mind, señor."

"I wouldn't miss it for the world," Carter said.

A very drunk man was hustled into the cab's back seat by a cold-sober hooker.

The cab drove away.

A gang of young toughs loitered out in front of the club. A bull-necked bouncer kept them from blocking the entrance but otherwise ignored them.

They greeted Xica's arrival with whistles and lewd remarks. Somebody flipped a cigarette butt that hit the pavement in a shower of embers near Carter's feet. Xica quickened her steps and tugged his arm to hurry him along.

A uniformed chauffeur who looked as if he could fill a front seat all by himself stood in the street with his hands on his hips. He loomed over the drunk who'd thrown a bottle at Carter's cab. The drunk was on his hands and knees, picking up the pieces of broken glass. The chauffeur encouraged him with an occasional kick.

Inside, the barnlike club was a scene of roaring chaos, smoky, noisy, hot, and dimly lit.

The bouncers knew Xica and waved her through.

"Where'd they get those guys?" Carter wondered. "They must have been recruited from a Ten Most Wanted list."

At one level, the Gato Negro was just another clip joint, with watered-down drinks, indifferent food, and worse service. On another level, it was a danger zone where the elite connected with the underworld.

The clientele was fairly evenly divided between the two. Slumming socialites rubbed shoulders with hardcore criminals, and not even Carter could always tell the two apart.

Above all, the nightclub was a marketplace.

"What's your pleasure, Markham?" Xica asked. "Whatever you want, you can find it here. Girls, boys, gambling, drugs—they're all for sale here."

"I want somebody to burn down a building for me."

"Don't tell me!" Auburn hair flailed Xica's shoulders as she shook her head. "I don't want to know about it."

"Right now, though, I'll settle for a table," Carter said.

"I see Yavar," Xica said. "We'll join him over there."

The place was too crowded for Carter to make out at whom she was pointing. He held her by the arm as they threaded their way between the jam-packed tables.

Xica stopped and put her mouth close to his ear. "Don't mention that we ran into Quintana."

"I won't."

"Yavar doesn't want any part of him."

A U-shaped area bounded the sunken dance floor and the stage. Yavar's table stood against the wall at the top of one of the U's vertical branches. He and his party shared a circular booth whose top was screened by long beds of potted plants.

Xica whispered, "The money?"

"Not yet," Carter said. "Why don't you give me the rundown on who's who?"

"Yavar's the one sitting in the middle."

"I figured that," Carter said.

It was easy. Xavier Yavar, contractor and middleman for Garcia Espinosa, was the only one of his party of five to wear a tuxedo. The tux and his rooster's comb of slicked-back hair were black and shiny as oil. The face below the pompadour was almost too perfect. He seemed deeply engaged in earnest chatter with his associates, but his watchful eyes saw Carter coming from a long way off.

A bosomy brunette with heavy false eyelashes and glossy pink lips sat on Yavar's right. His arm encircled the bare white shoulders of the long-haired blonde on his left.

Two men occupied the outside ends of the seat.

One was a rugged, balding man whose thick eyebrows and mustache framed a many-times-broken nose.

Xica identified him: "Virgilio Vasquez, Yavar's lieutenant. The piece of slime sitting on the other end is Tanango."

Tanango was young, in his early twenties. His eyes were set too close together and he had a loose, slobbering mouth. His head was dwarfed by his body-builder's physique.

Tanango saw Xica coming. He perked up and smacked his lips.

Xica said, "I don't know the girls. They don't matter."

"Why don't we all get acquainted?" Carter suggested.

Yavar rose and clasped Xica's hands across the table. "So glad you could join us, *corazón!*"

A surly waiter brought two more chairs to Yavar's table, and Xica and Carter sat down.

Tanango blew Xica a kiss. "Hey, baby!"

Yavar said, "Señor Markham, I presume?"

"That's me," Carter said.

"So nice to know you."

They shook hands. Despite the lounge lizard pose, Yavar kept himself in good condition. There was power in his grip.

"Allow me to introduce the rest of my little band of merrymakers."

Consuelo was the brunette, Sonia was the blonde. Consuelo was a bit tipsy and greeted Carter with a big hello. Sonia smiled wanly.

A bored Vasquez nodded his acknowledgment. Tanango sneered at Carter, then leered at Xica.

"Just what we needed to liven up the party—a redhead! Hey, Xica, honey, when are you going to let me find out if you're a real redhead or not?" Tanango said.

"I see you still haven't housebroken your pet monkey, Xavier," Xica said.

"What makes you so stuck up, huh?" Tanango demanded. "Since when are you so much better than everyone else?"

Yavar frowned at Vasquez. Vasquez said, "Tanango."

"Eh?"

"Shut up."

Tanango shut up and sulked. Looking for something to do, he noticed a matchbook. He tore matches loose from the pack and tossed them at the heavy bronze ashtray sitting in the center of the table.

An attentive waited appeared the instant that Yavar raised a finger.

"The usual, Xica?" Yavar asked.

She nodded.

"Champagne cocktail for the lady," Yavar said. "What's yours, señor?"

"Scotch, thanks," Carter said.

"And the rest of us will have another round," Yavar told the waiter, "except for him." He indicated Tanango. "He's already had enough to drink."

Tanango, chewing his lower lip, ripped out another match and shredded it into the ashtray.

When the waited returned, Yavar raised his glass in a toast. "Your good fortune, señor."

"I could use some," Carter said.

"Who knows?" Yavar drained his glass and set it down. "Your luck may have already changed."

"Let's hope so."

"I feel certain of it." Yavar leaned across the table. "I dislike shouting over the noise. With your permission, I know a more private spot where we can chat undisturbed."

Carter glanced at Xica. "I don't want to leave my charming companion for too long."

"Who could blame you? But we're not going far. Just upstairs."

"It's okay with me."

When Yavar rose, Sonia whined, "Xavier, where are you going?"

"We'll be right back."

"Take me with you—I want to go with you!"

"Such dreary business details would bore you to death, little one." Yavar patted her pink cheek.

He told Vasquez, "Give the girls some candy so they don't get bored while we're gone."

Vasquez nodded. He took a pillbox out of his pocket, set it on the table, and lifted the lid. The box was filled with white crystalline powder.

Sonia still had her baby fat, but the expression of greed and lust on her face would have done credit to a Borgia courtier.

She jumped up, threw her arms around Yavar, and pressed sloppy kisses on his face. He reached down to squeeze her round buttocks before disengaging himself.

"Me, too?" Consuelo said enviously.

"Certainly," Yavar said. "You too, Xica."

"I pass," Xica said.

"Oh?" Yavar lifted an eyebrow. "You surprise me. No matter. I'm sure you'll keep yourself amused until our return."

Carter followed him to an archway guarded by a tough-looking character.

"Man's a friend of mine. We want to talk on the stairs for a minute," Yavar explained.

"Go ahead," the guard said.

They passed under the archway and climbed two flights of stairs, halting on a dim landing lit by a bare red light bulb.

"Feel the music?" Yavar asked. "The sound comes right through the walls, but not so loud that we can't talk. So, let's talk."

Carter took out his cigarette case, then opened it. "Smoke?"

"Thank you."

Carter lit up, then held the flame to Yavar's cigarette until it ignited. "Marvelous thing, fire."

"Ummm."

"It solves all kinds of problems."

"How true." Yavar exhaled smoke through his nostrils. "And from what Xica tells me, you do have a problem, señor."

"A warehouse full of them."

"Tell me more."

"I represent a group of international investors," Carter began. "We buy good potential properties in depressed areas at bargain rates, renovate and reclaim them, then unload them for a nice fat profit."

"Fascinating." Yavar's tone implied it was anything but.

"A multimillionaire back in the States created a foundation to fund his favorite charity, an oceanographic institute. I got some inside information that the institute is looking for some waterfront property in Peru where they can build a research center. They plan to study the Humboldt current and El Niño, so they need a central location."

"And you found one."

"Right. Hell, I bought one," Carter said, "sight unseen. I'm not the boy to buy a pig in a poke, but this deal required fast action. On the map, the site was perfect. The price was a steal. There was just one little problem the seller forgot to tell me about before he took the money and ran."

"Yes?"

"Waste. Toxic waste. Hundreds of barrels of industrial pollutants are stored in my warehouse and on the pier."

"That is a problem," Yavar said sympathetically.

"I planned to demolish the building, but what do I do with the goddamned barrels?"

"You could dump them in the sea," Yavar suggested. "Or have them carted away."

"That's a big job. An expensive job. Too expensive for my profit margin to handle."

"I see."

"But if the place burned down, I'd be in the clear," Carter said.

"Accidents do happen."

"Yes. Especially with a little help. It's a big job and it's got to be done professionally. I can't even be rumored to be connected with it. The ecology freaks at the institute would never deal with me if they found out."

"May I ask you a question, señor?"

"Shoot."

"How did you happen to hear about me?"

"I get information the old-fashioned way," Carter said. "I pay top dollar for it. I put out some feelers to my local contacts and told them that I wanted the best in the business. They told me to get you."

"You flatter me," Yavar said. "You realize, of course, that I am only the contractor. I merely handle referrals, passing them along to my associate, who actually does the work."

"Just as long as he's the best. This isn't like burning down a house. This property is *big*. You know that newspaper building that burned to the ground a few weeks ago?"

Yavar was a little too casual. "I seem to recall something about it, yes."

"That's the kind of job I want. I want this warehouse leveled," Carter said. "I'll pay top dollar."

"Quality craftsmanship doesn't come cheap."

"I'll pay premium prices as long as I'm getting the best."

"I'm certain we can reach a mutually satisfactory arrangement."

"Time is important," Carter said. "This has to be done fast or not at all."

"I can't quote you any serious estimate until my associate has examined the property. The price varies according to the difficulty of the job."

"Can he come out tomorrow to take a look?" Carter asked.

"I don't see why not. Let's get together at, say, five o'clock?"

"Five is fine." Carter gave him the Callao address. "Aren't you going to write it down?"

Yavar tapped the side of his head. "It's all written down in here."

He handed Carter a business card that had his name and a Lima telephone number printed on it. "You can contact me through my answering service. Where may you be reached, in case of scheduling difficulties?"

"I'm staying at the Hotel Marsano."

"Lovely place. I know it well."

"I guess that covers everything for now," Carter said.

"One final word, señor. Our arrangement is not one that can be written down on paper, but once it is finalized, it is as binding a contract as any legal document. Considerably more so, in fact. You may cancel anytime before the final agreement is made, but after that, there can be no turning back."

"I understand."

"And, of course, the sum must be paid in full in cash." Yavar smiled thinly. "I'm sure your credit is excellent, but we don't accept checks."

"No problem."

"Excellent." Yavar tossed his cigarette butt on the floor and stubbed it out with his toe. "The ladies must be growing impatient. Shall we return?"

"Let's," Carter said.

EIGHT

When they returned to the main floor, it was noisier and more crowded than ever.

Yavar waved to somebody across the room. "I see some friends I haven't seen for a long time. I'll go and say hello. I'll join you at our table in a few minutes."

"Okay," Carter said.

Yavar joined a group of well-fed, well-dressed elderly gentlemen and their female companions. Carter tagged them as respectable businessmen enjoying a night on the town. The sleekly expensive ladies with them weren't their wives. They weren't their daughters or their grand-daughters, either, although they were young enough to qualify for those roles.

Whoever they were, they were no threat. They made room for Yavar to join them at the table.

Carter made his way through the jam of bodies. He sidestepped neatly, avoiding a collision with a waitress carrying a tray of drinks.

Vasquez was glumly shooing away a voluptuous club employee whose generous figure was poured into a black lace merry widow and a pair of fishnet stockings. She wore a Polaroid camera with a flash attachment around her pretty neck.

She was another money-making come-on for the club. "Souvenir photo of you and the lovely ladies, señor?" she cooed. "Only a few *sols* for a permanent memento of your fabulous night at the Gato Negro."

Consuelo and Sonia were all for it.

"We want to have our picture taken," Consuelo demanded. "Buy it for us, Virgilio!"

Sonia laughed giddily.

Encouraged, the photographer lifted her camera, but Vasquez waved her away.

"No pictures, I said!"

Carter grinned wryly. He could appreciate the hoodlum's aversion to having his picture taken. The last time Vasquez was photographed, he probably had a row of numbers under his chin as identification of the police files.

Tanango took advantage of Vasquez's preoccupation to crowd Xica. He was leaning all over her. He shoved his leering face within inches of hers. He tried to act suave but just looked stupid.

He slipped his arm around Xica's shoulders. She shrugged out from under it. He replaced his arm and pulled her close, his thick fingers digging into her flesh.

Xica squirmed, wincing with pain. Tanango laughed like a braying jackass.

He didn't see Carter standing behind him. But Xica acted before Carter was in motion.

Smiling sweetly, she pressed the glowing tip of her cigarette against the back of Tanango's hairy hand.

Bellowing in pain, he jerked his hand away.

"You bitch!"

Xica splashed her drink in his face.

Sputtering and wild-eyed, Tanango jerked his hand back to slap her.

Carter's hand covered Tanango's, bending the hoodlum's thumb inward in a vicious nerve pinch. Tanango bellowed, rising out of his seat in Carter's direction in an attempt to ease the painful pressure.

"Let me go, you bastard—owwwwwww!"

"Be polite," Carter said.

Eyes rolling, mouth gaping, Tanango gurgled in agony. A sob caught in his throat as Carter released him.

While everyone's attention was on Tanango, Carter's hand drifted over the table and found what it sought.

He said to Xica, "We'll be going now."

As she rose and moved behind him, she whispered, "Watch out! He'll come for you!"

Vasquez sat back and did nothing, but he seemed interested in Carter for the first time.

"I'll kill you!"

Tanango jumped to his feet, nearly overturning the table, spilling drinks.

Consuelo screeched and Sonia giggled.

Tanango's bull neck flared. Veins stood out on his red face. His thick arms lunged for Carter.

Tanango was wide open. Carter threw a wicked right that connected with Tanango's chin, splitting it.

The punch landed with a ringing metallic sound. Tanango's head slammed back. He crashed against the back of the booth, knocking one of the potted plants over onto the patrons at the adjacent table.

His eyes rolled up, showing their whites. His face went slack. He slid off the seat and slumped under the table, out cold.

A flashbulb popped. The photo girl recorded the scene.

Vasquez lowered his raised eyebrows. "That's some punch you got there, *hombre*!"

"Nothing to it," Carter said, surreptitiously ridding himself of the heavy bronze ashtray he'd palmed before the fight. It was dented where it had hit Tanango's chin.

Yavar hurried up. "What's happening?"

"Tanango had too much to drink." Carter straightened his black bow tie and brushed a speck off his lapel. "He's sleeping it off under the table."

"The American knocked him out with one punch!" Vasquez said.

Yavar raised both eyebrows.

"Hope I haven't spoiled your evening," Carter said.

"Not at all. I like a man who can take care of himself," Yavar said.

"We'll be running along. I've had as much excitement as I can stand for one night. Good night, all."

As Carter steered Xica past Yavar, he added, "See you tomorrow. And do me a favor."

"Name it."

"Leave Tanango at home. That is, if he wakes up by then."

"Don't worry. I'll straighten out that drunken clown," Yavar promised.

The crowd that had gathered to watch the short-lived fight made way for Carter and Xica to depart.

Vasquez lifted his head from under the table. "I can't wake Tanango."

"Leave him there," Yavar said.

He set off after the club photographer.

"I warn you, Markham," Xica said, "Tanango won't rest until he kills you."

"He's resting now," Carter chuckled.

He stopped laughing when a man moved away from the bar to intercept him.

"We meet again, Señor Markham."

"Hello, Quintana," Carter said. "I'd buy you a drink, but we're leaving, as you can see."

"Don't let me detain you. By the way, Señor Markham, have you a permit for that weapon under your arm?"

"You have good eyes, Quintana."

"It's my job to notice such things," Quintana said modestly.

Carter wasn't in the mood to be braced by a cop, not even a VIP in the national detective force.

"I forgot to apply for a permit," Carter said. "How much will it cost me?"

"You think I am sniffing around for *mordida*? For a payoff, as you *norteamericanos* so colorfully put it?"

"I confess that thought crossed my mind."

Quintana laughed. "No, no. That's not what I'm about at all. A man must protect himself, eh? Especially with conditions so unsettled in my poor country at this time. I'm not going to make an issue out of it."

"Thanks," Carter said. "That's awfully decent of you."

"But take care, señor. Few members of the police are as broadminded as I."

"I'll remember that."

"I won't keep you any longer." Quintana stepped aside to let them pass. "*Buenos noches, señorita*."

"Good night, Quintana," Xica said. "For the second time tonight."

"Until we meet again, Señor Markham."

Quintana stepped back and melted into the shadows.

"That fellow has the damnedest way of popping up where you least expect him," Carter said.

"His being here is no accident."

"I didn't think so."

"Make no mistake, Markham. He's got his eye on you."

"Nice of him not to get fussy about my gun, though." Carter held the door for her as they exited the club.

"He's not nice," Xica said. "He just can't be bothered with a little *mordida*. Quintana only takes the biggest bites."

"He'd better take care that he doesn't choke on them," Carter said.

NINE

The taxi drove to Xica's flat in Miraflores.

"You did your job." Carter passed her the second pay envelope.

When Xica slipped it into her purse, Carter glimpsed a shiny little pearl-handled pistol.

"Not counting the money?" Carter said. "Since when did you become so trusting?"

"I'll count it later," Xica said.

Night fog, Lima's famous *garua*, rolled off the ocean. Streamers of vapor crept through hushed streets, blurring the city lights into a palette of smudged pastels.

The cab halted in a square surrounded by two-story Spanish Colonial buildings.

Carter got out of the cab and went around to the other side to open the door for Xica. She swung her long legs out the door and stepped out onto the cobblestones.

"Thanks for a lovely evening," Carter said.

"You're coming upstairs, aren't you?"

"Our business is done, Xica."

"That's why I'm inviting you, Markham. Business is one thing; pleasure's another. Besides, I'm curious."

"About what?"

"I want to find out if you're as good as you think you are."

Carter smiled, then leaned over and paid the driver. "You needn't wait."

The court echoed hollowly to the sound of the taxi driving away. Its taillights became misty ruby globes before fading from sight.

Surf pounded somewhere in the distance. The air was damp and cool. Moisture glimmered on stucco walls.

Xica's second-floor apartment was luxurious. The walls of the sunken living room were covered with cloth of gold. Grass-green deep-pile carpet stretched from wall to wall. Massive overstuffed furniture was grouped around a stone fireplace, the pieces upholstered in expensive fabric. The space was subdivided by leafy green plants in large planters.

"Quite a place." Carter crossed the living room into a hallway. He opened the first door he came to. "What's in here?"

"I should have known you'd find your way there," Xica said. "That's the bedroom."

Carter reached into the dark room, found the light switch, and flicked it on.

The boudoir was even more opulent than the living room.

Xica came up behind him. "Do you always stick your nose where you're not invited?"

"Actually, I'm just checking to make sure there's no outraged husband lurking in the woodwork," Carter said.

Or an assassin, he thought.

It wasn't likely that he was being decoyed into a trap, but men die every day from the unlikeliest causes.

"The bar's in the living room," Xica said. "Make yourself comfortable. You could pour me a drink while you're at it."

Xica went into the bedroom, the door clicking shut behind her.

The bar cabinet was as big as a refrigerator turned on

its side. Carter hauled out a bottle of vintage pisco, Peru's excellent brandy, and splashed a liberal amount into a pair of snifters.

A long swallow of the potent beverage helped cut the night air's chill, but Carter decided that a fire would be ever better. He took off his dinner jacket, unslung his shoulder rig, folded the jacket over the gun, and laid it aside.

Not too far out of reach.

He rolled up his sleeves, piled some logs in the fireplace, found some old newspapers, and stuffed them under the logs for kindling.

The fire was crackling nicely when Xica returned.

Her tangled auburn mane and glowing skin were perfectly complemented by the emerald green lingerie molded to her lithe form. A pair of matching satin mules added inches to her height.

Silk and satin rustled when she moved. She was proudly aware of her sensuality and of the effect it had on Carter.

The fire warmed his body, the brandy warmed his belly, and the sight of Xica sent primal heat racing through his loins.

"You like my outfit?" she asked coyly.

"You're a vision, Xica."

She eyed him as intensely as he eyed her. "You're not so bad yourself, Markham."

He handed her a brandy and held on to his own. "Cheers."

"*Saúde*," Xica toasted in her native Portuguese.

She tossed back most of her drink in one gulp. Carter poured her some more, then sat down on the couch. Firelight outlined her leggy form as she moved between him and the fireplace.

He pulled her down onto his lap, her perfect bottom

nestling against his thighs, then he bent his head and kissed her. He tasted brandy on her tongue, along with subtler, sweeter flavors.

Their mouths locked, tongues tasting, teasing, probing. Her soft hands moved expertly over his neck and shoulders, caressing them.

He opened her negligee. Beneath it she wore a silk camisole and a pair of silk panties. Her body heat seethed through the lingerie. Her nipples were stiff points jutting against the shimmering fabric.

He stroked the tops of her breasts. Her skin was smoother than the silk that covered it.

Her long thighs quivered with excitement. They opened to Carter's touch. His stroking fingers glided steadily upward and she shivered as he touched her through the silk. Xica's eyes had closed and her open mouth moaned.

Carter eased Xica off his lap and onto the couch. Clothes were an obstacle to be gotten rid of as quickly as possible. A heap of his clothes and hers grew on the floor in front of the couch.

Xica looked up at him from where she lay, her long hair spread out across the colorful cushions.

"Markham . . ."

"Umm?"

"You *norteamericanos* are always in a hurry. Rush, rush, rush . . ."

"I suppose that's true," Carter conceded. He was in a hurry to strip off the last of his clothing.

"When it comes to loving," Xica breathed, "I need a man who takes his time."

"We've got the whole night, Xica."

She arched her back, lifting her bottom off the cushion so he could take off her panties.

She was a natural redhead.

Her arms were open and so were her legs as he sank onto the couch. Her skin was almost unbelievably smooth and hot.

She closed her eyes and moaned as he kissed her breasts. She stroked the powerful muscles of his arms and torso, and kneaded the small of his back.

He was ready, but he waited until she cried out for him, her eyes open now, pleading and eager.

Her fingers dug into his back as he entered her. Breath hissed through her clenched teeth.

Carter took his time. A body like Xica's was meant to be savored.

Sweat oiled their skin as they moved, perfectly attuned to each other's rhythms. Their senses feasted on the pleasures they gave one another. Their movements became fierce, excitement spurring them to greater efforts.

Eventually Carter could delay it no longer, and with his pulse throbbing in his brain, his breath rasping in his chest, he plunged into Xica for a last time, feeling himself go beyond time and place.

But wherever he was, she was with him, and they clung to one another until they fell to earth once again.

TEN

Leon Corona gave a lunchtime poetry reading at the Lima Cultural Center. An audience of twenty-five people was scattered throughout the 250-seat hall. A fifth of the group were homeless beggars who came in search of a clean place in which to sleep.

Corona read his verse with a booming, oratorical delivery. At times the beauty of his lines seemed to move him to tears, but that was only an illusion. Actually, his contact lenses were irritating his eyes.

The number of listeners decreased by half before he finished. All the beggars stayed until the end. The Cultural Center personnel had some trouble evicting them from the warm, well-lit hall.

When Corona stepped down from the podium, a lovely young coed rushed breathlessly toward him.

"Bravo, bravo! That was wonderful!" She threw her arms around him and planted a big wet kiss on his bearded cheek.

The poet's delight was spoiled when the girl whispered, "Yuri will meet you at the Govinda."

The Hindu Govinda at 149 Azangaro was a rarity, a vegetarian restaurant owned and operated by shaven-headed Hare Krishna disciples. Popular with the university crowd, the place was sparsely occupied when Corona arrived in midafternoon for his rendezvous.

"Yuri" sat alone at a secluded table set off by itself in

an alcove. A stolid, square-faced, middle-aged man, he had gray hair, a gray suit, and a gray complexion.

His real name was Konstantin Tyutin. A colonel in the KGB, he posed as a member of the Soviet trade mission department that handled his country's extensive arms trade with Peru.

Usually he passed the time with a few pleasantries, but today he got right down to business.

"I examined the pictures your courier brought me this morning," Tyutin said. "I didn't bother sending them along to Moscow for identification."

Tyutin laid a pair of glossy photographs face-up on the table, turning them so Corona could see them.

The first photo was one that Yavar had bought from the camera girl at the Gato Negro. Yavar's party was caught in the frame.

The second photo was an enlargement of a detail of the first. It showed a dark-haired, muscular, grim-faced man in a dinner jacket.

"Do you know who that man is?" Tyutin demanded.

"He calls himself Markham and he claims to be a businessman, but he's a mystery to me," Corona said. "That's why I sent the pictures to you."

"His name isn't Markham, it's Carter. Nicholas Carter. Does that mean anything to you?"

"Nothing."

"He's an agent of the American government. Part of a very secretive organization called AXE."

"What?"

"And he's not just any agent, either. He's one of their top operatives."

Corona paled.

"Carter is on our 'A list' of agents slated for termination if the opportunity presents itself."

Corona had recovered. "He'll be eliminated."

"He's been on our kill list for years," Tyutin snorted. "He's still alive, but the agents who tried to take him out aren't."

"Peru will be where his luck runs out."

Tyutin was skeptical. "I dare not supply you any backup. My network cannot risk showing its hand. If Carter learns that we're involved, the Apuchaka affair could break wide open. The consequences would be disastrous to one off our most important operations."

"What makes you think I need your help?" Corona asked. "My people will neutralize this man."

"As easy as that, eh? They laugh at fire who have not been burned. Carter's burned us before. If you're not careful, he'll do the same to you."

"He's in my territory now. I'll do the burning."

"I wish you luck. AXE's involvement means that serious measures have to be taken to minimize the potential damage of the Apuchaka affair."

"That sounds like you're passing sentence," Corona observed.

"I am, but you're the one who'll carry it out. We must be rid of everyone who can hurt us with revelations in this messy business."

Corona leaned forward. "Have you discovered who passed the information to *La República*?"

"No. That's out of my hands now. You'll have to find out—and soon."

It was Corona's turn to sneer. "You've really got the wind up over this man Carter."

"You would, too, if you knew what he can do."

"He won't live long enough for me to know him."

Tyutin rose. "I won't see you again until this matter is settled."

"Tell your chiefs in the Kremlin that they can cross Carter off their list," Corona said.

ELEVEN

Carter's appointment with Yavar and associates was scheduled for five o'clock in the afternoon. Carter arrived four hours early.

The sky was white with sea haze when Carter parked his car in a sheltered niche whose wall of barrels hid it from sight of the street.

Celia's people had supplied the vehicle. Carter decided against using them for active support. Celia was too valuable to risk, Cates was no shooter, and Villafirmo, while seemingly competent, was an unknown quantity. Carter had enough to deal with without having to worry about a teammate's safety.

He was ready for action. He wore a bulletproof Kevlar vest under a dark jacket whose pockets were stuffed with spare clips of ammunition.

Wilhelmina in hand, he prowled the site, poking into corners to ensure that nobody was waiting for him. The site came up clean.

Tying a bandanna over his mouth and nose for protection against toxic fumes, he ransacked the warehouse for potentially useful items.

A pile of oily canvas tarps could conceal the car. But something of far greater value sat in a dark corner: a forklift.

He climbed into the vehicle's bucket seat, wiped the controls clean with a rag, and tried to start it up. The engine sputtered, groaned, coughed, and failed to turn over. Carter opened the protective bonnet and shone his penlight beam into the guts of the engine. It was grimy and furred with dust.

The battery wasn't dead; it still held power. The fuel gauge showed there was more than half a tank of gas. Carter pressed Hugo into service, using the stiletto's needle-sharp point to scrape corrosion off the points. The carburetor came in for a cleaning too.

When he had done all he could do, he got behind the wheel and hit the starter.

The engine labored, knocking and shaking. Booming backfires rocked the vehicle. The engine caught and turned over, roaring into life. Blue-gray clouds erupted from the exhaust.

Carter grinned as he engaged the gears and wheeled the forklift around the piles of barrels. Handling like a bumper car, it was capable of surprising speed.

Carter halted at the big metal sliding door and dismounted. A rusty chain and pulley system cranked the door upward after Carter applied some muscle to it.

He drove the forklift out to the end of the pier, soaking up great gulping breaths of fresh air. Exposure to gas and chemical fumes in the warehouse had left him light-headed.

When his head cleared, he went back inside and scooped up the pile of tarps on the lift, driving them to his car's hiding place.

Unfolding the tarps, he covered the car with them, then stepped back to examine his work. After making a few more adjustments, he was satisfied that the camouflage could stand up to a casual inspection.

He repeatedly shut down the forklift and started it up again. He had to be certain it would come alive if and when it was needed.

The forklift passed the test. Carter drove it behind the guard shack that stood to one side of the locked main gate.

Then he settled in to wait.

With any luck, greed for a lucrative job of arson would lure Espinosa out of hiding to meet "Markham." If he failed to show, Carter would still have Yavar. The Killmaster had no doubts that he could neutralize Yavar's bodyguards and "persuade" him to reveal Espinosa's whereabouts.

The guard shack provided the perfect blind for keeping the street under surveillance. The size of four phone booths combined, it was topped by a slanted roof. The side facing the pier was open, its door having fallen off at the hinges. The other three walls each had a narrow window, supplying vantage points.

Inside the shack was a table and two chairs. Carter positioned a chair so he could see through all three slitlike windows.

He sat down and waited for his guests.

They arrived at three o'clock.

A light blue van cruised slowly down the street. Carter ducked down and watched it over the top of the windowsill.

Chugging along at a few miles per hour, the van rolled past the site. It went to the far end of the street, rounded the corner, and drove out of sight.

A few minutes later, two men emerged from the street that the van had taken. Elaborately nonchalant, they strolled down the avenue, halting in front of the main gate of Warehouse 535.

One of them was a thin youth, the other an older man in a yellow short-sleeved shirt.

The youth sidled up to the gate, holding a key ring filled with master keys, picks, and shims. He whistled as he worked on the lock. The yellow-shirted man stood in front of him, smoking a cigar, shielding his partner from the view of chance passersby.

The youth stopped whistling. A click sounded as the padlock was picked open.

Crouching low, Carter ducked out of the shack and took cover behind the forklift.

The youth entered the site, shutting the gate behind him so it would appear that no one had tampered with it.

Yellow Shirt stayed in place, standing with his back to the gate while he smoked his cigar and kept watch on the street.

The youth approached the shack with exaggerated stealth and peered inside it. A toothy grin split his beardless face when he saw it was empty. He pressed the stud on his switchblade, retracting its eight-inch blade.

He didn't know Carter was hiding a few feet away from him.

Carter could have taken him out then, but that would be premature. Not all the guests had arrived yet. He knew they would be coming soon.

The youth moved along the pier with wary intensity. He glanced at the niche where the car was hidden but didn't bother to look under the tarps.

He entered the warehouse but didn't spend much time prowling through it. The fumes must have gotten to him, since he staggered out coughing and choking.

He hurried back to the gate to report to his partner. "All clear!"

A coughing fit wracked him. He brushed tears from his eyes.

Yellow Shirt grinned. "What's the matter with you?"

"God, it stinks in there!"

"I thought maybe you were crying for the poor *yanqui*."

"He's the one who'll be crying," the youth said.

"Here they come."

The van cruised into view. Yellow Shirt gave them the high sign, signaling that all was well.

He and his partner opened the gate wide as the van drove up. Vasquez drove and Yavar rode in the passenger seat.

The van entered the yard, reversed, and backed into a spot diagonally across from the shack. A wall of barrels hid it from the street. It faced outward for a quick getaway.

The engine shut off and Vasquez and Yavar got out of the cab. Even in the weak light of a cloudy day, Yavar looked pale and pasty.

Vasquez pounded on the wall of the van. Its rear door opened and two men got out.

They looked tough and competent. One carried an automatic rifle loaded with a banana clip. The other cradled an M-1 machine pistol in his arms.

"Fix the gate," Yavar ordered.

The youth and Yellow Shirt shut the gate. The youth slipped a thin arm between the space where the gates met and snapped the padlock back into place.

"He'll never know we got here first," Yellow Shirt said with a harsh laugh.

The machine gunner asked, "What do we do now?"

"We wait," Vasquez said.

"If Carter's smart, he'll get here early," Yavar said.

"If he's smart, he'll stay away."

"He thinks he's got us fooled, but he'll find out who's the fool." Yavar consulted his wristwatch. "You men will get into position by four o'clock. As soon as Carter's inside, cut him down."

The Killmaster swore under his breath, wondering how Yavar had learned his identity.

"This sure is a lot of firepower for one man," the rifleman said.

"That's what I say," Vasquez grumbled. He brandished a long-barreled .45 revolver Wild West style. "Hell, I'll do the job myself with this!"

"This is how the chief wants it," Yavar said.

"He could have saved his money."

"What do you care, Vasquez? It's his money, not yours."

"Yeah," the rifleman joked. "What have you got against us making a few sols?"

Yellow Shirt kicked a barrel. "What kind of shit is in here, anyway? It stinks to high heaven!"

"I hope we don't have to wait too long," the youth said.

"Why don't we take him alive?" Vasquez suggested. "That way we could have some fun with him before we kill him."

"Nothing fancy. Just shoot him and be done with it," Yavar said. "Besides, the man is tricky. Look at how he handled Tanango last night."

"I wish I could have seen that," the machine gunner said and grinned.

"Too bad Tanango's not along on the job," Yellow

Shirt said. "I bet he'd like to pay that *yanqui* bastard back for spoiling his face."

"Don't waste your time feeling sorry for Tanango. He's the lucky one. He gets to take care of that treacherous Brazilian bitch," Vasquez informed them.

They all broke up laughing.

That changed everything. Carter had planned to wait until the group separated to their positions and then pick them off one by one. It would have been good to take Yavar alive for questioning.

That plan was now defunct.

Earlier that day, he'd warned Xica that it would be a good idea for her to drop out of sight for a while. She wasn't inclined to take his advice. She laughed and said she could take care of herself.

Carter wasn't going to abandon her to Tanango's tender mercies.

Reaching into his pants pocket, he pulled out a Pierre-type mini-bomb. Now was the time to act, while the ambushers were bunched together.

He thumbed down the red arming button. The tiny grenade had a five-second delay between arming and detonation.

He counted under his breath: "One one thousand, two one thousand, three one thousand—"

Leaning out from behind the forklift, he rolled the grenade across the pier toward the van.

As he ducked back under cover, he heard somebody say, "Hey, what's that?"

Somebody else yelled inarticulately.

He was silenced by the explosion of the powerful little grenade.

Carter hopped onto the forklift and hit the starter.

After a blood-chilling pause, the engine fired up with a roar.

The breeze blowing in from offshore dispersed the smoke on the pier, revealing a scene of mayhem.

Yellow Shirt lay sprawled in a pool of his own blood. Beside him was his partner's mangled body.

The rifleman had dropped his weapon and held his hands over his face, screaming as he staggered blindly. He looked as if he had run into a buzz saw.

The machine gunner jumped up from behind the barrels that sheltered him. They leaked vile fluids from dozens of holes, but he was unhit.

He opened fire, squeezing off a burst of slugs that bounced off the heavy-duty steel of the lifting gear at the front of the forklift.

Pistol fire erupted from under the van, where Yavar had rolled before the grenade went off. His right arm was useless. He shot with his left hand, his bullets flying wide of the mark.

Vasquez crouched in the cab of the van, shooting with one hand while he tried to start it up.

Carter threw the forklift into gear and charged the machine gunner, who stopped shooting and started panicking as the vehicle bore down on him.

The forklift slammed into a wall of barrels, crushing the gunman beneath them.

Yavar had found his range. One of his shots breezed through Carter's hair.

The Killmaster reversed, backing away from the over-turned barrels.

Vasquez had flooded his engine. He bellowed with fear-ridden rage as the forklift came toward him on a collision course.

The forklift hit the van broadside, its extended steel forks plowing through it above the rocker arm. Metal crumpled like tinfoil.

After the impact, there was an instant's resistance where neither vehicle moved.

Carter worked the gearshift and floored the gas pedal. The forklift bulled forward, shoving the van ahead of it.

Yavar crawled frantically, trying to drag himself clear. His upper body cleared the van. He still held his pistol but was too busy moving to do any shooting.

The van's right front wheel went over Yavar's midsection. His agonized scream ended in a choked gurgle.

The forklift powered the van to the edge of the pier.

Vasquez bounced around the cab. He grabbed the door frame with both hands and started to lever himself free just as the van tilted backward.

Vasquez was thrown against the driver's side door.

Carter leaped clear as the van went over the side into the water, taking the forklift with it. He hit the ground rolling, coming up on one knee with Wilhelmina in his hand.

No one was left to oppose him.

He wasn't certain that the machine gunner was finished off for good, so he cautiously approached the jumble of barrels. The choking fumes from the spreading pool of chemical wastes were almost overpowering.

The machine gunner was dead. Pinned flat by a pile of barrels, he'd drowned in the toxic fluid.

Yavar was the worst. The crushing wheel had squeezed him in the middle like a tube of toothpaste.

The greasy gray-green water boiled with air bubbles streaming up from the sunken vehicles. Carter waited a minute, but Vasquez didn't come up.

Carter pulled the tarps from his car, hopped in, and started it up.

Wheels whirled, laying a patch of rubber as the Killmaster stomped on the gas pedal and shifted into high gear.

The car leaped forward, smashing the gates open. It hurtled down the street in a blur of speed.

Xica's apartment in Miraflores was twelve miles away.

Vasquez clung to a slippery piling under the pier. Seawater spilled from his nose and mouth as he gasped for breath.

When he heard Carter drive away, he swam to shore.

He knew what had to be done. There was still a chance to stop the American agent, if he could reach a phone in time.

TWELVE

Xica's apartment door was open. Carter smelled gunsmoke.

Crouched low with his Luger in hand, he ducked inside, panning for targets.

He found none.

A big body stretched facedown on the floor, blood leaking from its head into the beige carpet.

Carter approached cautiously. He wedged his foot under the corpse and flipped it over onto its back.

Tanango's sightless eyes stared at the ceiling. A bullet hole had been drilled through the center of his forehead.

"Well, I'll be damned!" Carter muttered.

He crossed the living room into the hallway. A door at the far end of it stood slightly ajar.

Was it his imagination, or did the door open another fraction of an inch?

Flattening himself against a wall to get out of the direct line of fire, he called softly, "Xica?"

He heard something moving.

"Xica? It's me, Markham!"

A pearl-handled pistol poked its snout out of the door. The door swung open.

Xica huddled in the closet, holding her gun with both hands.

Carter wasn't going to startle her into pulling the trigger, but he wasn't going to lower his gun, either. Xica was a variable, an unknown quantity.

"That was a nice bit of shooting," he said in a conversational tone.

"I told you I could take care of myself, Markham."

"The police may think that you do it too well. Suppose we leave before they get here?"

"That's a good idea." She lowered the gun to her side.

Carter exhaled the breath he'd been holding.

She came out of the closet and he went to her. She was wild-eyed and shaken, but otherwise unhurt.

"I'd feel a lot better if you put the safety on that gun," he said.

"Why should I trust you?"

"Right now, I'm the only one you can trust, Xica. Between Tanango's pals and the police, you're in big trouble."

"There's no crime in defending myself. Besides, I wouldn't be in trouble if not for you."

"You played the game and took the money. With playmates like Yavar and Tanango, it was only a matter of time before something like this happened. But that's water under the bridge now. What's important is to get out of here before more troops arrive."

"You're right, Markham." She leaned against a wall. She looked tired. "Yavar will never rest until I'm dead."

"He's resting now. Permanently."

That cheered her up.

"You did it? Maybe I backed the winning side after all."

"Why don't we discuss it somewhere else? I'd prefer not to play questions and answers with the law," Carter said.

Xica snapped the safety into place on her pistol. She

shuddered once, and then she was all business.

"You have a car?" she asked.

"Outside. Let's hurry. I'm double parked."

She smiled thinly. "Always with the jokes, eh, Markham? Or is Markham your real name?"

"The name's Carter. Nick Carter."

He watched her carefully, but she betrayed no sign that the name meant anything to her.

"Nick Carter," she echoed. "One name's as good as another. Very well. We'll go on the run together, Nick Carter."

She ducked into her bedroom.

"Now what?" Carter growled.

Xica hauled a suitcase out of a walk-in closet and tossed it on her bed.

"There's no time for packing," Carter protested.

He was anxious about the open door, the dead man, the neighbors, the police, Yavar's friends.

"There's always time for money," Xica said.

Kneeling in a far corner of the room, she lifted the carpet, peeling it back. She pressed a hidden stud and a lid opened in the floorboards.

Below lay a combination safe bolted to a structural beam. Xica twirled the dial and opened the safe.

"The suitcase, Carter."

Carter set it down beside her.

She plunged her hand into the safe and came up with a fistful of jewelry, which she tossed into the bag. She hauled out another handful, and another.

"If those are real, you're a very wealthy woman."

"They're real. I always go first class, Carter."

"If you don't hurry, you can use them to pay off the police."

"Almost done."

The gem supply was exhausted, but she still hadn't

reached the bottom of the safe. She fished out two fat blocks of big-bill currency and added them to the loot.

She dropped the pistol into her handbag, hefted the suitcase, and said, "Now we go."

"Hallelujah!"

Carter took her arm and hurried her into the living room.

He went to the window, lifted the curtain, and looked outside.

A small knot of neighbors gathered in the square, talking fast and pointing excitedly at Xica's apartment. Carter listened for the wail of police sirens but didn't hear any.

He started to turn away from the window when the squeal of tires made him look again.

The spectators scattered like birds taking flight as a taxi zoomed around the corner on two wheels and roared into the square.

Coming straight on toward the building, it braked hard and went into a skid, rear-ending a parked car—not Carter's, luckily.

Its doors were flung open and four armed men in ski masks jumped out.

"Is there a back way out of here?" Carter demanded.

"Yes, but—"

"Let's take it. Move!"

He followed her into the kitchen, where she tore open the locks and bolts on the back door.

"Who are they?" Xica cried.

"Yavar's pals!"

Footsteps pounded up the front stairs. They were close—too close.

Carter decided to even up the odds.

He dashed into the hall just as the first masked man hurtled through the door.

Carter put two shots into his chest.

Mortally wounded, the masked man toppled sideways to the floor. His gun was forgotten as he tried to hold back the flow of his life's blood with both hands.

The second man had thrown himself behind the cover of the wall when the first was shot. His head and gun hand flashed in the doorway as he pumped some rounds in Carter's direction.

Plaster chips and dust gouged from the wall by bullets sprayed Carter, but he was unhurt.

He squeezed off a shot that thudded into the door-frame two inches from the masked head. The head ducked back behind cover before Carter could plant a follow-up shot in the right place.

The time factor was vital. Carter couldn't let himself be pinned down when there were two more shooters on the loose.

He fired two more blasts through the door to discourage pursuit and dodged into the kitchen.

Motioning Xica to silence, Carter flung open the back door and slammed it shut.

A heartbeat later, the killer at the front door charged inside, deluded into thinking that Carter and Xica had gone down the back stairs.

He ran into the hallway and into a bullet from Carter.

He tumbled backward as if he were trying to turn a reverse somersault.

Carter checked the back way. It was clear, but it wouldn't be.

Xica stood with her pistol in one hand and the suit-case in the other.

"Wait here!" Carter told her.

The back stairs clattered under his feet as he rushed to the landing at their midpoint. He dropped into a combat crouch, holding Wilhelmina at arm's length in both hands for accuracy.

The third and fourth masked men rounded the corner and came into range.

The fourth man was smarter than the third. He let his partner take the lead while he hung well back.

The third man's technique was sloppy. Shouting wildly, he emptied the better part of a clip as he rushed the stairs. He threw plenty of lead but forgot to aim.

Carter didn't.

He squeezed off a well-placed shot and the third man dropped.

The fourth and wiser man didn't offer much of a target while he lagged back to see what effect his companion's crazy charge would have.

He ducked behind the wall a split second before Carter's next shot ripped a crater in the stucco.

Carter vaulted the rail of the landing, dropping eight feet. He hit the ground rolling, then lay prone with the gun in his hand, waiting for the next target.

Blood bubbled out of the third man's mouth as he brought up his gun. He looked very young where the openings in his mask bared his face.

He wouldn't get any older. Carter gave him the coup de grace right between the eyes.

Footfalls raced away from him. The fourth man, wisest of all the masked killers, decided that he'd had enough.

He jumped into the taxi and fled the scene.

Carter didn't bother to give chase. He and Xica made their getaway.

The police arrived in force fifteen minutes after the shooting stopped.

THIRTEEN

Martin Santiago drove the stolen taxi like a madman.

He knew the streets of Lima, but Miraflores was alien territory to him, a confusing maze of avenues, boulevards, side streets, alleys, and culs-de-sac.

He was so flustered by the disastrous shoot-out that he turned into a one-way street and drove down it the wrong way.

He took a savage joy in the horrified faces of the drivers coming in the opposite, legal direction. Their cars peeled off to the left and right to dodge his hurtling machine. More than one of them rode up on the sidewalk to avoid an imminent head-on collision.

It seemed only moments ago that he'd received a frantic telephone call from Vasquez giving him the bad news about the massacre at Warehouse 535 in Callao. Santiago couldn't believe that one lone man had wiped out Yavar and all of his gang but one.

"You can still catch him if you hurry," Vasquez told him. "I'm sure I know where he's going!"

Santiago jotted down Xica Bandeira's Miraflores address and promised he'd be there right away.

Speed was of the essence. He didn't have time to round up a professional hit team, and he wasn't going after Carter by himself.

The only men he could get hold of immediately were

the members of Los Hidalgos. A phone call to a bar near the university campus turned up three of the brethren.

He told them he'd pick them up in ten minutes. He tossed some pistols and ammunition in a bag. Rifles and machine guns would have been better, but handguns were all he had. He could have gotten heavier weapons if only there had been more time.

He hailed a taxi. Its driver got out of the cab in a hurry when Santiago shoved a gun in his face. Santiago pistol-whipped him into unconsciousness to prevent his reporting the theft to the police.

The three Hidalgos knew that something big was up when Santiago's taxi screeched to a halt in front of the bar. They piled into the cab and it took off.

Santiago fed them the cover story:

"I just got a hot tip on a Red assassin, one of the Communists' top triggermen. He's fleeing the country, but if we act fast we can get him!"

His stooges bought the story without question. They were thrilled. They'd committed violence in the cause of Church and Country, but they'd never done the big job.

They'd never killed a man.

They were eager to remedy that lack. Guns and masks were pulled out of the bag and distributed.

They were children of privilege and knew the expensive suburb of Miraflores. Santiago followed their shouted directions.

It wasn't as if they were totally green. Carlos and Miguel both knew guns, and Felix had won medals in marksmanship competition.

But target practice on the range wasn't the real thing. Targets don't shoot back.

This one did, too well.

Now the three Hidalgos were dead, and Santiago was caught in a web of unfamiliar streets.

He hoped they were dead. God help him if one of them lived to identify him as the ringleader of the brotherhood!

He reached the end of the one-way street and zipped through an intersection, trailing angry horns and car crashes behind him.

A few blocks more, a cunning returned to remind him that such reckless driving could only attract the attention of the police.

He turned off the boulevard, slowing to a normal pace. No car pursued him.

Escape seemed possible. He started working on an alibi to explain to Corona why he failed to kill the *yanqui* spy.

Santiago drove another half mile before he thought to remove his mask.

FOURTEEN

Carter contacted Celia Rinaldi at AXE's Lima station. His pay-phone call was routed into one of her secure scrambled lines.

Before he could tell her the latest developments, she said, "Something's up, Nick."

"You don't know the half of it."

"Your Markham cover is blown."

"Do tell."

"I've been tied up all afternoon fielding calls from Guy Dean, CIA's chief of station at the embassy. He's furious. He knows who you are and he demanded to know what you're up to."

"What did you tell him?"

"Absolutely nothing, of course. I stonewalled all the way and denied I'd ever heard of you."

"That's how to handle him," Carter said.

"Dean's not a bad sort and usually we get along quite well. He wasn't acting like himself. I got the impression he was feeling the heat himself, and I was right. Ten minutes after I got rid of him, McLarran was on the phone."

"The ambassador? Where does he fit in?"

"I'd like to know that myself. He and Dean are the only embassy personnel who know who I am."

"What did McLarran want?"

"He read me the riot act, Nick. He demanded to know what kind of operation you're running. He was outraged that it hadn't been cleared with him, whatever it was."

"Everybody wants to get into the act."

"I told him what I told Dean. That is, I told him nothing. Then I contacted Hawk. He's got the clout to handle this kind of bureaucratic infighting."

"What did the old man say, Celia?"

"He was more intrigued than upset, but there was no doubt that he's definitely annoyed by the interference."

Carter chuckled. "There are going to be some red faces at the Company and at State when Hawk gets done telling them off."

"In the meantime, Dean's people can make things rather uncomfortable for you, Nick."

"They're the least of my worries. How hard are they crowding you?"

"I'm catching a lot of flak on the administrative level, but it's only a power play. All very civilized. They may very well try cruder tactics on you."

"I've got some news that puts Dean and McLarran in their proper perspective," Carter said.

He gave her a quick rundown of his busy day.

"Good God!" she said when he was finished. "You sure do make things happen!"

"Life should never be dull," Carter said dryly.

"What a coincidence that everyone discovered at the same time that George Markham is not what he seems."

"Yes," Carter drawled, "isn't it?"

"What next, Nick?"

"I need a safe house to stash Xica before we get her out of the country."

"There's one in Surquillo not far from an airport."

"Sounds goods."

Celia gave him the address and the recognition code for admittance. "I'll notify them to expect you."

Carter didn't have to worry whether the location was known to CIA chief Dean. An AXE safe house is kept secret from all outside parties.

"Thanks a million, Celia. I've got a few ideas I'd like to kick around with you later."

"You know where to reach me."

"The game's getting rough, luv. Watch yourself."

Carter said good-bye and hung up.

He got back in the car with Xica and drove south along the coast for a few miles.

"Carter . . ." Xica said.

"Umm?"

"I have to tell you something."

"I'm listening."

She worried a loose thread on her dress before continuing. "I told Quintana about you . . . about Markham, I mean."

"That doesn't surprise me," Carter said evenly.

"It doesn't?"

"Meeting him once could have been coincidental . . . not that I believe in coincidences. But somebody must have told him we'd be at El Gato Negro, and it wasn't me. That left you."

"You're not angry?"

"I'm not thrilled, but I can live with it. Maybe now you'll tell me where he fits into the picture."

"I gave some cocaine to a friendly acquaintance. Gave, not sold. It was just a little, and he was so insistent . . . . What harm could it do?"

Her mouth twisted bitterly. "My friend was one of Quintana's spies. Quintana arrested me. If I worked for him, he said, he'd drop the charges. If I refused, he'd arrange for me to draw the maximum sentence in prison.''

She shuddered. "I could never survive prison, Carter. I'd cut my throat first, before the other inmates did it for me.''

"So, you cooperated."

"I became another of his spies."

"What's his game?" Carter asked. "Who's he working for?"

"Himself."

"What's his interest in Yavar and Espinosa?"

"He's obsessed with catching the man who burned down *La República*. He thinks Espinosa is that man."

"And when he catches him, what then? Will he bring him to justice or shake him down for *mordida*?"

"Only Quintana knows the answer to that question." Xica shrugged. "He's a crooked cop who hates criminals. He might do both."

"Squeeze him for a payoff and then turn him in?"

"Or kill him. Quintana's a killer, too," Xica said.

Carter had to laugh. "You sure got yourself in with a nice crowd."

He made the turnoff and went north on the Pan-American highway toward Surquillo.

Xica slumped in her seat. "Now I'm on the run with another killer. I'm so tired of running."

"Don't bite the hand that strokes you. This run will take you all the way to Cancún, Mexico."

"Are you serious?" She stared at him.

"You've overstayed your welcome in Peru, Xica. It's time to move on. I suggested Cancún because it's your kind of place, but you don't have to go there. You can go where you please. Hell, you can even go back home to Brazil if you like."

"Oh, no, I can't!"

"Too hot for you there, huh?"

"Why do you think I came to Peru in the first place?"

"You can tell me all about it when we're lolling on the beach in sunny Mexico."

"Carter, if this is another one of your jokes, I'll shoot you!"

"It's no joke. It'll take a day or so to get the arrangements squared away. Then you'll be on a plane saying good-bye Lima, hello Cancún."

"Where will you be?" she asked suspiciously.

"I'll be staying on here for a week or two to tie up some loose ends. Then I'll join you for a well-deserved vacation."

"Unless they kill you."

"You're a cheery soul."

She put her hand on his shoulder, squeezing it gently. "Nick . . . why are you doing this for me?"

"I guess I'm just a pushover for wayward girls."

FIFTEEN

Señora Ada's brothel sat on the north bank of the Rio Rimac, not far from Lima's Desamparados railway terminal. The two-story dive did a thriving business in booze, dope, and girls. The girls got used up quickly, but there was an endless supply of them to be had from the masses of peasants who had abandoned the countryside for the promised land of the city.

The girls turned their tricks in rooms upstairs, on the second floor. The ground floor was a long, low space stocked with crude tables and chairs and cruder customers.

Tonight it was doing a roaring business.

Clouds of tobacco and marijuana smoke fogged the air but failed to disguise the compounded reek of sweat, booze, and cheap perfume.

The madam herself looked like a truckdriver in drag. She was a no-nonsense woman who did most of the bouncing. Backing her up was Ayala, her dandified fancy man, a fast hand with a straight razor or a gun.

Señora Ada lined up four of her girls and put them on display. Two were meaty and stolid. The other two were rail-thin drug addicts.

"Well, gentlemen, who will it be?" Ada asked. "Who's the lucky girl?"

"None of those pigs," Espinosa spat.

"We want something fresh," Ugarte said.

"Don't be so picky, boys." Ada chucked a beetle-browed woman under her double chin. "Show them your pretty smile, Carmen. You see, she has all her own teeth!"

"If you want her to keep them, get her out of my sight," Espinosa said.

"She's not to your liking? What about Lola? Now, here's a woman who's a real handful! Look at those tits! Big as melons and twice as juicy!"

Espinosa said, "What do you think of her, partner?"

Ugarte was looking elsewhere, staring at a slim young girl who carried a tray of drinks. She couldn't have been more than fifteen years old. She glided gracefully between the tables, dodging the clutching hands that tried to grab a feel of her rounded rump and her small, firm breasts.

Espinosa saw her, too.

"Mmmmm," he said, "we haven't had that one before."

"Rosalita's new," Ada said. "You don't want her. She's just a green kid who doesn't know the score yet."

"We'll break her in for you."

"She's not used to the rough stuff—"

"Better and better," Espinosa said, laughing.

Ada looked worried. "I have an investment in that girl . . ."

"You'll be well rewarded, as always."

Espinosa lit a fresh cigarette from the butt of his previous one, which he tossed away. It smoldered in the sawdust floor at Ada's feet. She stared at it, open-mouthed.

Expinosa stamped it out. "Can't be too careful with fire, eh?"

Ada shuddered.

"Get the girl, *amigo*," Espinosa said.

Rosalita served foaming mugs of corn beer to a group of rowdy construction workers. Ugarte caught her by the arm.

"Come here, little bird."

One of the workers, a big hard-faced bruiser, growled, "Wait until she's done giving us our drinks."

Ugarte pulled the tray from her hands and slapped it onto the table, spilling some beer. "She's done now. Let's go upstairs, pretty one."

Rosalita winced as his grip tightened on her arm. "Please, señor, you're hurting me—"

"I would never hurt you, angel. Let's go."

The bruiser pushed his chair back from the table and rose. He stood only a few inches shorter than Ugarte, and he was built broader.

His four friends readied to back his play.

"Hey!" the big man shouted at Ugarte.

"You got a problem?" Ugarte demanded.

"No," the bruiser replied, "you're the one who's got the problem."

"That's telling him, Pablo," one of his pals chimed in.

Pablo was playing to an audience, since the other patrons craned their necks to observe the byplay.

"You come over here like you own the place. You spill our drinks, and you pester the señorita," Pablo said. "Who the hell do you think you are?"

"I'm the man who's going to knock you down." Ugarte grinned malevolently.

Pablo grinned too. "You can try."

Ugarte walloped him with a big right hand. Pablo flew backward, crashing into the table and knocking over all the drinks.

His friends jumped up, beer-drenched and cursing.

Pablo recovered his footing. He rubbed his jaw as he

shook his head to clear it. "If that's the best you can do, you're in big trouble!"

"Break him, Pablo!" one of his friends said.

"Hell, I'll break him myself!" another snarled. "The bastard!"

All four moved to assist Pablo. They hadn't taken more than a few steps before a shot rang out.

They halted in their tracks.

A wisp of smoke curled from the muzzle of Espinosa's deadly little pistol.

"Shut up, sit down, and stay alive," he suggested quietly.

One of Pablo's friends said, "You can't shoot us all, pipsqueak. One of us will get you—"

Espinosa fired casually, from the hip.

The man who had spoken cried out in pain, clapping a hand to his bleeding ear. Espinosa had shot off its lobe.

"Next time, I take the whole ear," Espinosa said softly, and smiled.

Ada looked at Ayala. Ayala's hand inched toward the pistol stuffed in his waistband.

"Uh-uh," Ugarte chided, shaking his head and wagging a finger.

Ayala's hand dropped to his side.

Ugarte grinned.

The man with the bleeding ear slunk to his seat and sat down. The others followed, Pablo last of all.

"Smart," Espinosa said approvingly.

His gun swiveled to cover a newcomer who had just entered. He eased his finger off the trigger when he saw who it was.

"Santiago!" he exclaimed. "What are you doing here?"

"He hasn't come to get himself a woman," Ugarte

teased. "Not Santiago. He hasn't got any use for them. You should have been a priest, Santiago."

Santiago sniffed. "I don't sleep with dirty whores."

"Your father did," Ada cracked.

"What's up?" Espinosa asked.

"There's work to be done," Santiago said.

Ugarte and Espinosa looked at one another, then back at Santiago.

"What are we doing hanging around this pigsty?" Espinosa said. "Let's go!"

Ugarte released Rosalita. Whimpering, she rubbed her arm where purple bruises marked the imprint of his gripping hand.

"Some other time, my pretty little flower," he cooed.

Espinosa bowed mockingly to Pablo and friends. "This is your lucky night, *amigos*."

He fired twice, blasting a leg off Pablo's chair, spilling the big man to the floor.

"Something to remember me by," he said.

He and Ugarte followed Santiago out into the night.

SIXTEEN

Lima's early-morning rush-hour traffic scattered the *garua*, replacing it with a smog of automobile exhaust. Carter entered the Hotel Marsano.

He was temporarily out of leads but not out of action. He was now a target. He decided to show himself and see what that stirred up.

He went in by the front entrance. The uniformed doorman nodded, saying *"Buenos dias, señor."*

"Buenos dias."

The lobby was bright, cheery, and largely empty. One of its few occupants was a crew-cut athletic man whom Carter instantly tagged as an American.

The well-built man sat at the far side of the lobby, filling an armchair that commanded a view of the entrance. He held an open newspaper but wasn't reading it.

When he saw Carter, he concealed his face behind the paper.

Carter didn't give him a second glance. He crossed the lobby and climbed the stairs to the mezzanine. When he had passed out of the sight line of the seated man, he doubled back, using a row of columns to cover his move.

The American put aside his paper and hurried to a row of pay phones. He made a call, spoke a few sentences, and hung up.

He entered an elevator and rode it up to the third floor.

When he got there, Carter was waiting for him.

The American moved down the hall toward Carter's room. Carter stepped out from behind the door to the stairs, where he'd been hiding.

The American heard something behind him and started to turn. Carter jabbed his index finger into the man's back.

"Hands at your sides, nice and easy, unless you want to catch a bullet right here," Carter warned.

When the American's head jerked around to look over his shoulder, Carter poked him harder.

"Face front!"

"You—you won't shoot," the American blustered. "Not right here in the open."

"Try me. Get against the wall."

"Listen, you—"

"Do it!"

The American assumed the position, facing the wall, hands pressing it at shoulder height.

Carter gave him a fast pat-down frisking and relieved him of a Walther PPK. He used it in place of the finger he'd been pressing against the other's back.

He relieved him of his wallet, too.

Carter flipped it open and read the ID. "Gary Wing, CIA. Hands down, Wing. Move."

"Where?"

"We'll take a little walk to my room. That's where you were going anyway. And don't get cute."

They started down the hall, Carter following close on Wing's heels.

"You won't shoot, Carter. Not here, in a public place."

"If you know who I am, you know I'll shoot. Nobody'll kick up a fuss about the loss of a junior-grade field op like you, Wing."

"You're in deep shit, you know that, man?"

"Maybe, but I'm the one with the gun."

As they neared the room, Carter said, "How many inside, Wing?"

"Nobody—hey!"

Carter had just poked him with the gun muzzle. "Try again. If anything goes down, you'll be the first casualty, Wing."

"There's one guy inside."

"Only one?"

"That's all, I swear!"

"His name?"

"M-Milo. Milo Herrold."

They halted a few steps from the door. Carter flattened against the wall.

"No tricks, Wing. If you're thinking about tipping off your partner, think about this instead."

Carter poked him again.

Wing knocked on the door. No reply came from within.

"I doubled back and left the hotel," Carter whispered.

Wing chewed his lips. He knocked again. "Milo! It's me, Gary! Open up, will you?"

After a pause, the door was unlocked and opened. A gruff voice said, "Where the hell did he go?"

"He doubled back and left the hotel—"

Carter propelled Wing forward with a hard shove. Wing hurtled through the doorway, crashing into a middle-aged, shaggy-haired heavyweight.

Carter bulled into the room while Wing and Herrold

were entangled. He kicked the door shut while covering them both with the Walther.

Herrold angrily shoved aside Wing. "What the hell!"

Herrold had made himself comfortable during the stakeout. His jacket was off, his tie was loose, and his sleeves were rolled up.

Herrold wore a .38 Special in a side holster worn high on his hip.

"I'll take that." Carter moved behind Herrold and put the Walther to the back of the agent's hairy head. He freed the revolver from its rig and pocketed it.

"Dumb," Herrold snarled at his partner. "Dumb, dumb, dumb!"

"I—I couldn't help it," Wing stammered. "He got the drop on me!"

"Stupid son of a bitch," Herrold snapped. He turned to Carter. "And you're another one."

"That's why I'm holding the gun and you're under it," Carter noted.

"Not for long, chum, not for long."

"You boys go sit down with your hands behind your head and your backs to the wall," Carter commanded. "Move!"

Herrold and Wing obeyed, sitting on the floor.

Carter hauled his suitcase out from under the bed and laid it open on the mattress.

"Time for me to move along," Carter said. "Too many undesirable elements in this hotel."

Keeping them covered, Carter cleared his clothes out of the closet and stuffed everything into his bag. He packed one-handed, keeping the gun in his other hand.

"You can run but you can't hide," Herrold said.

"I'm shaking."

"Laugh while you can."

"Tell Dean to send some pros after me next time," Carter said.

"Dean?" Herrold sneered. "We don't work for that piss-ant. Brock's our chief."

That gave Carter pause. "Brock?"

"You've heard of him, huh?"

"I sure have," Carter said.

Brock was a power in the CIA's Western Hemisphere Division, covering Latin-American operations.

He'd also been a player in the Apuchaka affair twenty years ago, Carter remembered.

Herrold misinterpreted Carter's reaction. "Now you're getting smart. You don't want Brock mad at you."

"Keep those hands behind your head," Carter snapped when Herrold lowered them.

"You're not getting smart after all," Herrold said with a scowl.

"I'll talk with Brock," Carter said.

"You sure will. He's come a long way to have that chat and he doesn't like to be disappointed."

"He's here in Lima?"

"Yeah. He sent us to pick you up. Now how's about giving us back our guns and we take a little ride?"

"Not a chance," Carter said.

"Shit, you're dumber than Wing here."

Carter picked up the phone.

"Who're you calling?" Herrold asked.

Ignoring him, Carter told the front desk to connect him with the American embassy. When the call went through, he demanded to speak to Guy Dean.

He smoked a cigarette while waiting for Dean to come on the line.

"Dean here."

"Nick Carter here. This line is open, so watch what you say."

A pause. Then: "Listen, Carter, you're in—"

"No, *you* listen. I've got two clowns here named Herrold and Wing."

"Who're they?"

"They claim they're working for Brock."

"Steve Brock? Are you serious?"

"I am, but I'm not sure that they are. They also say that Brock's here in town."

"Ridiculous. He's in Washington."

"You know that for a fact, Dean?"

"Well, no, but I haven't heard anything about that."

"You're hearing it now. Sounds like Brock's poaching on your territory."

"He wouldn't dare! He—" Guy Dean paused to get hold of himself. In a voice deliberately calm, he continued, "This isn't something we can talk about on the phone."

"I agree," Carter said. "I want a meeting between you, me, and Brock. I'll contact you later to arrange the details."

"Wait a minute—"

Carter hung up.

"Thanks a lot for putting us in the shit," Herrold breathed.

"My pleasure."

"I'm not forgetting this."

Carter dropped Herrold's gun into his suitcase, closed the lid, and locked it.

Herrold shouted, "Hey, what are you doing?"

"I'll pass your guns along to Dean. You can get them back from him."

"Thanks," Wing said glumly.

Carter hefted his suitcase and carried it to the door. He pocketed the Walther.

The lack of a gun in Carter's hand didn't encourage Wing to try his luck. He stayed in place.

"Stick around, boys. Relax. Call room service," Carter said. "Check-out time's not until noon." He went out and walked down the stairs to the lobby, alert and wary.

No suspicious characters lurked in the lobby, and the sidewalk and street seemed clear.

A taxi pulled up to the curb in front of the hotel awning, disgorging an elderly couple who couldn't be anything but innocent tourists. The doorman unloaded their bags from the trunk and followed the couple inside.

Carter got into the taxi's back seat. "Plaza San Martin."

"*Sí, señor.*"

A stream of oncoming traffic pinned the taxi at the curb. The driver stuck his head out of the window, searching for an opening.

The traffic light changed at the corner behind them, halting the flow of cars.

The taxi began nosing into the lane.

Somebody leaned on a horn and kept leaning on it. Frowning with annoyance, Carter glanced out the rear window.

More horns honked and brakes screeched as a Mercedes truck ran the red light and bore down on the cab.

"What's he doing?" the driver gasped.

The taxi wouldn't get clear in time. Carter flung the door open and dove to the sidewalk.

Launching himself headfirst, he rolled his shoulder under him, somersaulted, and jumped to his feet. He was still scrambling when the crash came.

The cabbie screamed as the trucker yanked his steering wheel hard to the right and plowed into the taxi.

The side of the taxi crumpled from the tremendous impact, spraying glass as it imploded.

The truck shoved the taxi up over the curb and across the sidewalk. It swept up a pair of luckless pedestrians, hurling them through the plate glass windows into the lobby of the Hotel Marsano.

There were screams, shouts, the clatter of falling glass, and the hiss of pressurized steam escaping from the taxi's cracked radiator.

Carter was unhurt, except for skinned palms and knees.

The cabbie wasn't so lucky. What remained of him looked like raw meat oozing out of a crushed tin can.

The trucker hopped down from the cab of his vehicle. He wore a workingman's cap and a brown jacket. He ran across the street.

Unable to shoot for fear of hitting an innocent bystander, Carter gave chase.

The trucker didn't have such concerns. When he reached the other side of the street, he hauled a gun into view and spun to confront the Killmaster.

Carter jumped back to avoid a speeding green sedan. He glimpsed four tough-looking men inside.

Swerving clear of the Killmaster, the green sedan made a screeching U-turn in the middle of the street and zoomed forward in the opposite direction.

The trucker forgot about shooting and started running. He wasn't far from the corner. For an instant, it looked as if he might make it.

The green sedan hopped the curb and sped along the sidewalk.

Its right front fender smashed the trucker, smearing him against a brick wall.

The sedan kept on going. Its heavy-duty suspension took the shock as it bounced back into the street.

The driver jauntily tooted the horn. The sedan rounded the corner, shot forward, and disappeared from sight as it hurtled down the avenue.

The best part of the trucker looked like a bloody rag doll, but his agonized face was intact.

Carter didn't recognize him.

The scene of destruction was a magnet for the curious. Spectators hurried to see the carnage.

There was no point in trying to retrieve his suitcase from the devastated taxi. It contained nothing incriminating, with the possible exception of Herrold's .38, and that was the CIA man's loss.

Carter moved off, putting some distance between himself and the Hotel Marsano.

When the Killmaster was safely gone, Virgilio Vasquez stepped out of his vantage point inside a recessed doorway opening on the intersection.

"Lucky bastard!" he spat.

Carter had escaped, but that wasn't important. He was a walking dead man, and it was only a matter of time before the outfit settled up with him.

What was important was that Vasquez had recognized the men in the green sedan that had plowed the truck-driving assassin.

"The Mesa Verde gang!" he breathed.

Why were those bastards sticking their noses in business that didn't concern them?

Whatever the reason, Corona had to have the news fast.

SEVENTEEN

Celia Rinaldi's chauffeur and bodyguard was a locally recruited AXE operative named Ramirez. Squat and taciturn, he expertly guided the bulletproof armored limousine up the hairpin curves of the road to Ambassador McLarran's villa high in the foothills of the Cerro San Cristobal.

Behind and below them lay the city lights and, beyond that, the broadly curving void of the Pacific.

Carter and Celia rode in the back.

"Quintana's a power," Celia was saying. "He has the support of some very important people in the oligarchy."

"Important enough to cover up eight kills?" Carter asked.

"Eight, or eighty. Or eight hundred," Celia said. "What mystifies me is why he's suppressed all information about your involvement in the shootings at the warehouse and at Xica's apartment."

"I'm sure he wouldn't do it without a good reason."

"That's what mystifies me."

"Maybe he smells a buck in it," Carter suggested. "Or maybe he likes to see rebels and hoodlums gunned down."

"Whatever his motivation, I'm grateful for it. Otherwise, you'd be the object of a nationwide manhunt right now."

112

"That could be it," Carter said. "He might be doing some manhunting of his own, using me as a stalking horse to flush out his prey."

"Quite possibly."

"I'm glad Xica's safely out of the country. Quintana will just have to get along without her."

"That reminds me," Celia said. "A message came in over the wire as I was leaving the station for this meeting. Your friend arrived in Cancún without incident and is now safely ensconced in the Marina del Sol hotel."

"That's good news. Who's holding down the station tonight, Celia?"

"It's Cates's turn to stand watch, but I doubled the guard. Alfonso's sharing the watch with him."

"I feel better with Villafirmo on duty."

"So do I," Celia said. "If I weren't so short-handed during this crisis, I'd send Cates packing."

"Car behind us," Ramirez said.

A pair of bobbing headlights climbed the road a half mile back.

Carter loosened Wilhelmina in her holster for a speedier draw. The weight of mini-grenades in both pockets was a comfort, too.

Ramirez maintained his speed. The other car made no effort to cut the distance between them.

A yellow glow shining up ahead where the road leveled off was the lights of McLarran's villa.

The house sat on a flat rocky shelf. It was ringed by a high stone wall topped with razor-sharp concertina wire. High-intensity lights glared inside and outside the walls, banishing darkness that could conceal invaders. A hundred-foot zone surrounding the walls was cleared of all scrub brush for the same purpose.

Ramirez slowed to a halt outside the gate. A guard in

civilian clothes emerged from a door in the wall and approached the driver.

While Ramirez identified himself and his passengers, Celia recognized the car that rolled up behind them.

"It's Guy Dean," she said.

Carter removed his hand from the butt of the Luger and rested it on his leg.

The guard verified their credentials and signaled to an inside man to open the gate.

The limo rolled into a vast courtyard. The gate closed behind them while the guards checked out Dean.

A horseshoe-shaped driveway led them through lush gardens to the front of the long, sprawling, stucco-walled house.

Ramirez opened Celia's door. She and Carter got out of the car.

A guard dressed like a butler came out of the house to escort them inside. His domestic livery clashed with his gunbelt and holstered sidearm.

"This way, please."

"Just a minute," Carter said. "Let's wait for Dean."

Dean's car pulled up alongside the limo, and the CIA's chief of station in Lima climbed out.

A pudgy blob of a man, Guy Dean was overfed, overtired, and out of shape. "Good evening, Celia."

"Hello, Guy."

He gave her a polite peck on the cheek and turned his attention to the Killmaster.

"So you're Carter." He grinned toothily and stuck out his hand. "Glad to know you."

"Why?" Carter asked, giving Dean's hand a shake.

Dean pitched his voice confidentially low and spoke with feeling. "Any enemy of Brock's is a friend of mine."

"I thought you were on the same side."

"Hell, we're all on the same side, for what that's worth. That doesn't mean I have to take it and like it when Brock and his goons throw their weight around on my turf. I didn't even know he was down here until you told me."

"Brock's a long way from home," Carter prompted.

"Shit! . . . Pardon my French, Celia, but I'm so god-damned steamed. Brock's a Potomac desk officer. Hasn't been in the field for years. I don't know what he's doing mucking around on my beat, but I damn well mean to find out!"

"Go carefully," Celia cautioned. "I understand that Brock carries a lot of clout with the White House."

"Screw that! His big-shot pals on the National Security Council don't scare me. I'll be around long after the current administration is gone."

"Not if you continue making such intemperate remarks."

"You're right, Celia, you're right, but I'm hopping mad! I mean to get to the bottom of this!"

Dean checked again to make sure that the guard was still out of earshot. Lowering his voice, he asked, "By the way . . . what is this all about?"

"Why don't we go in and find out?" Carter said.

"An excellent idea," Celia seconded.

They followed the escort into the front hall, under an archway, and through a long narrow corridor. At its end stood a pair of ornately carved wooden doors with oversized wrought-iron handles.

The guard held the door open for the trio, closing it behind them from outside.

They were in a spacious anteroom. A pair of green leather armchairs flanked a floor lamp. The chairs were occupied by Gary Wing and Milo Herrold.

Brock's men jumped up when they saw Carter.

Carter said to Dean, "These are the two ops I told you about."

Wing was embarrassed; Herrold was enraged. The shaggy-haired man's face reddened and his bull neck swelled as he confronted Carter.

"Where's my gun, you bastard?"

"Lost," Carter said.

"You son of a bitch! That cost me plenty! Somebody's going to pay for that!"

"Why don't you send Brock the bill?"

"Very funny." Herrold squared his shoulders.

"Easy does it, Milo," Wing said weakly.

"Shut up." Herrold challenged Carter: "You got lucky with that sucker punch. Why don't you try to take a poke at me when I'm ready, you dirty—"

Carter was a blur of motion as he moved forward and popped a right to the point of Herrold's outthrust chin.

Herrold went from belligerent to inert in a split second. Carter grabbed his arm and hustled him into an armchair. Herrold slumped in it, unconscious.

"That was a hell of a punch!" Dean enthused.

"Nick, really!" Celia admonished.

The inner office door opened and two men came out.

The first was a sleek greyhound of a man. He had silver hair, white eyebrows, and a pencil-thin gray mustache. He was Sheridan McLarran, the United States ambassador to Peru and the host for tonight's meeting.

The second was Steve Brock. He was broad-shouldered, big-bellied, and wide-bottomed. His naturally red face went a few shades darker as he took in the scene.

"What's going on here?" Brock's flabby jowls quivered with indignation.

Dean couldn't resist giving him the needle. "Your

man's lying down on the job, Brock,'' he said, deadpan.

McLarran's patrician face expressed shock.

Brock went over to Herrold. "He's out like a light. What did you do to him, you bastard?''

"Nothing much," Carter said innocently.

"See here," McLarran scolded, "I won't stand for violence in my house. This is supposed to be a serious meeting, not a schoolyard brawl!"

"Come on, come on, wake up!" Brock shook Herrold, then slapped his face a few times.

Herrold moaned but failed to come out of it.

Spying a glass of water on the table, Brock picked it up and dashed its contents into Herrold's face.

Herrold's eyes flickered open. They were out of focus and so was his brain. He said thickly, "Whuh—wha' happen?"

"That's what I'd like to know," Brock said. "Snap out of it, for Chrissake! Wing, get him out of here and squared away!"

"Yes, sir."

Wing helped Herrold to his feet and supported him. Herrold shuffled along on wobbly legs as Wing led him from the room.

"I'd like to know how you did that," Brock said through clenched teeth. "Milo's one of my best boys!"

"You should get some new boys," Carter said.

"Send them back to Washington," Dean advised. "And go with them."

"I don't have to take that from you, Dean!" Brock said.

"No? You're way out of line, Brock! What the hell are you doing here anyway?"

"Gentlemen, please!" McLarran appealed to reason. "Why don't we all just lower our voices?"

"An excellent suggestion, Mr. Ambassador," Celia said. "When it's quieter, perhaps we'll hear some answers."

"Everyone, please, step into my study," McLarran said.

The group filed through the door. Carter let Brock go ahead of him. He didn't want Brock behind his back.

The study's tan stucco walls contrasted with its dark brown rough-hewn wooden beams. Tall bookcases housed hundreds of handsome leather-bound volumes.

A sideboard held bottles, glasses, mixers, and ice.

"Perhaps a drink will cool tempers down," McLarran said.

He and Celia selected sherry, Brock had bourbon, and Dean and Carter had scotch.

McLarran sat down behind an old carved desk as big as a pool table. The others occupied high-backed chairs grouped in a semicircle before it.

"Enough with the niceties," Brock said. "Let's get down to brass tacks."

"Yeah, let's," Dean said. "What the hell are you doing here, Brock?"

"Your job. You're sure not doing it."

"What's that crack supposed to mean?"

"Figure it out," Brock said.

McLarran cleared his throat. "There's no sense in all of us working at cross purposes. We're all after the same thing."

"And what's that?" Celia inquired.

"Finding out who killed Ed Dunninger," Brock stated.

"Why do you think he was killed?" Carter asked. "His plane crash could have been an accident."

"You don't believe that; I know I don't. Twenty

years ago I thought Ed was the victim of a conspiracy. I'm more sure of it now than ever."

Celia leaned toward Brock. "You worked with Dunninger at that time. You must have some theory about the identity of his killer—or killers."

"Sure, I had theories," Brock said bitterly, "lots of them. I couldn't follow them up. After Dunninger vanished, so did the suspects. Then the bridge was blown up, and the Apuchaka affair went into Washington's file 'em and forget 'em hopper."

Brock drained his glass of bourbon. "Only I didn't forget. Ed Dunninger was the best friend I ever had. I swore to even up the score no matter how long it took. It took twenty years, but the time has come."

He turned his hot-eyed gaze on Celia, Dean, and Carter. "Somewhere there's a clue in this twenty-year-old mystery that'll lead me to the killer. I'll find it no matter what it takes, and nobody'd better get in my way."

"Ever hear of working through the proper channels, Brock?" Dean asked.

"I'm authorized to conduct my own investigation."

"Authorized? By whom? Your pals on the National Security Council?"

"That's right," Brock said smugly.

"The deputy director of operations says I'm in charge."

"He's got no jurisdiction over my department."

"Why not work together instead of bickering over who's in charge?" Celia said.

Brock and Dean stared at her as if she were crazy. Finally Brock said, "What's it to you? I don't see where AXE figures in this at all."

Carter looked at his watch. The time was a few

minutes short of nine-fifteen.

He laughed out loud.

"What's so funny?" Brock demanded.

"You'll find out any minute now," Carter told him. "The message was transmitted from Washington at nine o'clock local time."

"What message?"

"The cryptographic computers at the embassy will decode it almost instantly. I figure it will take fifteen minutes or so for his staff to relay the message to the ambassador."

"What message?" McLarran asked, mystified.

"Don't listen to that double-talk," Brock said. "He's giving you the runaround."

There was a discreet knock at the door.

"That must be it now," Carter said.

McLarran said, "Come in."

A guard entered the room. "Call for you from the embassy, sir. On the scrambler line."

"Thank you."

The guard saluted, pivoted on his heel for an about-face, and exited, closing the door behind him.

"Excuse me, please." McLarran, puzzled, opened a door in the wall behind his desk and went through it.

"What are you trying to pull?" Brock demanded.

"I'll let the ambassador tell it," Carter said. "It'll be more convincing coming from him."

He went to the sideboard to refill his glass with scotch.

A few minutes later, McLarran returned. He looked surprised.

"Well, what is it?" Brock was exasperated.

"Please don't bark at me, Steve. Especially when you've heard the news," McLarran said.

"What news?"

McLarran sat down. "That was the code clerk at the embassy. They received a top-priority communiqué from Washington at exactly nine o'clock."

"Who sent it?" Dean asked.

"The Oval Office. The president has stated that AXE's authority in the Dunninger investigation supersedes all others."

Brock exploded. "The hell you say!"

"We are requested—ordered, actually, although the text doesn't put it quite that baldly—requested to extend all necessary cooperation and assistance to the AXE officers heading said investigation, those officers being Ms. Rinaldi and Mr. Carter."

"I don't believe it!" Dean said.

McLarran looked down his long thin nose at the CIA chief of station. "I'm not in the habit of having my word doubted, Guy."

Dean sighed. "I wasn't calling you a liar, Sheridan, I was merely expressing my amazement."

"Pretty slick," Brock said grudgingly. "How the hell did you work that power play, Carter?"

"I didn't. David Hawk did," Carter told him. "When it comes to power plays, Hawk wrote the book."

Ambassador McLarran spread a relief map of Peru on his desk.

He pointed out a red star set high in the Andes mountains. "Here's Cuzco."

Once capital of the vanished Inca empire and now Peru's second most important city, Cuzco lay inland some four hundred miles southeast of Lima.

His finger marked off another location two hundred miles east of Cuzco.

"Here's Puerto Maldonado, a key trading post on the

Madre de Dios branch of the Amazon River. It stands in the Amazon basin, jungle rich with fertile land and mineral wealth. The Apuchaka project was designed to link these two vital areas by rail. A lifeline to open the jungle for development. The railroad was a great dream and a tremendous engineering feat that had every chance of success."

"Until the Reds threw a monkey wrench in the machinery," Brock added sourly, his voice slurred. He'd been hitting the bourbon hard since he got the news from Washington.

"The railroad was being built simultaneously from both ends. They would meet at the midpoint, at the Tucuman gorge northeast of Quince Mil. That was the major stumbling block, trying to span the Inambari River at the gorge."

"That's where the project ran into a brick wall," Brock said.

"Spanning the river at the gorge was the toughest job imaginable. It almost failed for lack of funds, but Washington was keen on the project. We believed that it would win the hearts and minds of the people whom the leftists were trying to incite to Marxist revolution. Working through the Alliance for Progress, we channeled millions and millions of dollars into completing the Apuchaka bridge. And it was completed, or almost completed.

"Unfortunately, there was a political dimension to be dealt with. I saw it while serving as a junior foreign service officer, and Brock and his CIA people saw it too."

"The Reds were up to their usual tricks," Brock said. "They knew the project would work, and that's the last thing they wanted. They were dead set against anything that might boost the peasants' standard of living and delay their lousy revolution."

His voice was slurred but his steps were steady as he went to the sideboard for yet another refill.

"Man, you wouldn't believe the shit they pulled trying to derail the project," Brock went on. "They salted the work force with their organizers and agitators, and really went to town. They hit us with slowdowns, work stoppages, and strikes. When those didn't work, they came back with violence and sabotage. We were hurting."

"And then Dunninger stepped in," Carter said.

"Damn right. Ed the superspook, the expeditor, the man who gets results. He got 'em, too. Best goddamned operative I ever had the privilege of working with. When he and his pal Kelly went to work, the Reds never knew what hit 'em."

"But they hit back hard."

"Ed ran his own network of informants in the work gangs. He discovered an inner cell of saboteurs. The last time I saw him, he was ready to lower the boom on the wreckers."

"Only they got to him first."

"Yeah. They killed Ed, and two days after that, they killed the bridge. Blew it sky-high with enough dynamite to level a mountain. Total loss."

"Tell me about the conspiracy to kill Dunninger, Brock," Carter said.

"Oh, they were smart, all right. They had it all figured to a T. The night before Ed got on the plane, some goons jumped his sidekick in a bar and put him out of action with a beating. Buzz Kelly was Ed's right arm. With him out of the picture, there was nobody to cover Ed's back."

"Did Kelly have any lead on the plotters?"

"No. He was the muscle, while Ed did the thinking for both of them. They were a great team, but Ed never told Buzz anything he didn't need to know. Never told anybody else, either, including me. Buzz and I did plenty of digging afterward, but we never came up with anything solid."

"What about the mechanic, Fierro?"

"There's no doubt in my mind that he rigged the plane to crash. He serviced the planes at the airfield. That gave him the means and the opportunity. The motive? Money, what else?"

"Fierro was the plotters' tool."

"Yeah. They paid him off permanently. Buzz and I found his corpse a week later. Somebody'd emptied a forty-five into his belly."

"A hard way to die," Carter said.

The prospect pleased Brock. He grinned wolfishly.

"The killer must have hated Fierro as much as we did. But he was only a pawn. The big guys were covering their tracks."

"Don't forget to tell him about the woman," McLarran said.

Brock splashed more bourbon into his glass and sat down. He looked tired.

"You tell him, McLarran. She was on your staff."

Carter frowned. "You're referring to Dolores de la Parra?"

"You've done your homework, Mr. Carter," McLarran said. "Yes. Dolores was an exceptionally capable young woman with a fine family background. Quite attractive, too. She had been educated abroad and wanted to make a career of some kind before settling down. She was fluent in Quechua, the language of the highland Indians. Her contributions were considerable."

"She and Dunninger were lovers, I believe."

"You *have* done your homework," McLarran repeated. "I don't pry into the personal affairs of my staff as a rule, but their relationship was fairly obvious. It's easy to understand the attraction on both sides. He was in the prime of his life and career, a powerful and important man. She was young, intelligent, and very beautiful.''

"They got her, too," Brock said.

"Yes, they did. Dolores performed some clandestine investigations for the colonel. Her contacts with the Indians were extensive, and they made up the majority of the work force."

"She disappeared before Dunninger," Carter pointed out.

"Two days before he boarded the plane. At the time, I never suspected that she'd met with foul play. Neither did Dunninger—at least he said nothing about it to me. Steve knew him better than I."

Brock shook his head. "Not a word. He was edgy and quick-tempered those last two days, but I figured it was the hunt for the saboteurs that was getting on his nerves. It wasn't until a long time later that I got a crazy hunch about the whole deal."

"What hunch, Brock?"

Brock leaned forward, resting his forearms on his meaty thighs, his head drooping.

"See if this makes sense to you, Carter. What if Dolores were a plant—a Red spy?"

"Impossible!" McLarran declared flatly. "That's absurd."

Brock waved his hand. "No, no, hear me out. Suppose she was working for the Communists. It'd be child's play for a gorgeous broad like Dolores—lemme tell you, Carter, she was a knockout!—to make a middle-aged guy like Ed fall for her like a ton of bricks."

"I'm listening."

"There she is, working with him, sleeping with him, spying out his secrets and reporting them to her case officer. Ed's hot on the trail of the wreckers and they've got to stop him. Dolores throws a big scene. Maybe she tells him she's in trouble. She drops out of sight. Ed's frantic. She contacts him, tells him she loves him and can't live without him. She's waiting for him—in Lima."

"I'm still listening," Carter said.

"The one thing we could never figure out is just what the hell made Ed charter a private plane to Lima. It makes sense if you figure it this way. Dolores was the Judas goat. She lured Dunninger on the death plane."

"I don't believe it. I *can't* believe it. Dolores adored Dunninger," McLarran said.

"How do you know it wasn't an act?" Brock demanded. "The honey trap's the oldest gig in the world. It's stuck around because it works!"

Dean shook his head and broke his long silence. "What an imagination!"

"How about it, Carter?" Brock tilted toward the Killmaster. "What do you think of my hunch?"

"It's worth considering," Carter said. "It fits the facts as we know them."

"As opposed to the facts we don't know," Celia added. "There are too many of them in this case."

"It's your headache now." Brock laughed so hard that he spilled his bourbon. "You wanted to take charge of the case and now you've got it. Let's see if AXE can succeed where everybody else failed!"

EIGHTEEN

The antique store did not reply.

"I don't like this, Nick." Celia hung up the car phone. "They're not answering."

"We'll find out what's wrong," Carter said.

Ramirez whipped the limo through Lima's nighttime traffic, trailing a chorus of angry horn-honking.

They approached an intersection. The light changed against them, flashing red.

Ramirez held down the horn and ran the light. A car missed their rear bumper by inches.

Celia's face was calm, but she squeezed Carter's hand tightly.

"Maybe we should put on our seat belts," Carter said.

"We're slowing down." Celia leaned forward to speak to the driver. "Ramirez, what's wrong?"

"We can't go any farther. It's all jammed up."

"Pull over!"

The limo nosed in toward the curb. Carter had the door open before the car stopped rolling.

The trio followed the Colmena for two blocks, then entered the side street where the shop was located.

Red light tinted the overcast sky. The firelight came from a burning building.

"Oh, no!" Celia started to rush forward.

Carter caught her by the arm. "Let's not run in blindly. This could be a trap meant for us."

Ramirez thrust his hand in his jacket pocket, gripping his gun. His restless eyes scanned the crowd gathering to watch the blaze.

The antique store glowed with a hellish light. Smoke poured out of it. The inside of the shop was a mass of flames. The larger works of art were black silhouettes in the fire storm.

"The blaze can't have been going long," Carter told Celia, "or the crowd would be bigger."

"Maybe Peter and Alfonso got out," she said softly.

"Maybe."

The number of spectators grew by the minute. They ringed the scene at a safe distance, scrambling for position, dodging this way and that for a better view.

They surged as close as they dared. A uniformed policeman herded them back, but they kept coming closer.

"Look!" a man shouted. "There's somebody inside!"

A shadow writhed in the flames. The shadow was a man. He ran straight into the display window and bounced off.

"My God!" The policeman charged the shop, recoiling from the heat. He tore at the front door but couldn't open it. He rammed the glass with his nightstick but couldn't break through.

Overcome by the heat, he collapsed. Two spectators grabbed his arms and pulled him away from the fire.

The burning man grabbed a heavy chair and slammed it against the glass. His second attempt sent cracks through the glass. A third try, and the glass frosted and went opaque, shards spilling to the sidewalk.

On his fifth and last try, he used himself as a battering

ram and dove headfirst into the window.

He crashed through, a shrieking human torch.

Screams came up from the crowd as they backed off.

The burning man staggered a few feet forward and collapsed. He sprawled facedown on the pavement.

Carter tried to push forward but the crowd was packed too thickly for him to make any progress.

Somebody had the presence of mind to use a coat to beat out the flames wreathing the burning victim. Another fellow joined in.

The policeman sat up, coughing and choking. "The door . . . stuck . . . couldn't break it open . . ."

The broken window fed the flames with fresh oxygen, fueling it to new frenzy. Blackened glass imploded. Yellow-red sheets of fire swept over the façade.

Helping hands reached to haul the burned man clear from the blaze. He wasn't on fire anymore but was still sizzling. The helpers wrapped coats around their hands, grabbed the victim, and dragged him farther from the fire.

The asphalt where he had fallen was marked by a smoking, melted, man-shaped outline.

Not only women screamed when the charred body was brought into the light.

Celia, sickened, rasped, "It's Cates."

"How do you know?" The victim was so badly scorched that Carter had trouble telling if it was male or female.

"The shoes."

One of the victim's shoes had fallen off in the street. It had been a stylish loafer decorated with a small metal chain across the top. The leather was seared and the chain was half melted.

"Cates wore shoes exactly like that," Celia said. "I

think I'm going to be sick.''

Ramirez crossed himself and muttered a prayer.

Carter looked away from the body.

The faces of the crowd expressed fear, pity, and horror. But there were two individuals who showed quite different emotions.

Carter's gaze fastened on them.

It was easy to spot the big man. He stood a head taller than everyone else.

The little man who stood beside him was revealed when a gap opened in the crowd.

They both watched the fire with shining eyes.

A whirlwind of embers whipped out of the blaze. The duo looked at each other and grinned maniacally.

''Espinosa and Ugarte,'' Carter said.

''What?'' Celia looked left and right. ''Where are they?''

''There!''

But when Carter pointed at the spot where he'd seen them, they were gone.

''Stay here! Ramirez, watch her! There could be more of them!''

Carter bulled his way through the crowd, making free use of his elbows and knees. Each second's delay was agonizing.

His barrelling through the crowd nearly kindled a riot. A woman he shouldered aside hit him with her handbag. A man threw a punch that glanced off Carter's shoulder.

When he finally broke free, Espinosa and Ugarte were on the other side of the street, scuttling away. They had a fair head start, but Carter thought he could overtake them, and he ran into the street.

His pounding footfalls alerted them. They turned to see who was chasing them.

Carter reached for his gun. If only he could wing one of them . . . .

A fire engine swung around the corner with sirens wailing.

Carter jumped back to keep from being run over.

The big red machine screeched to a halt. Firemen jumped down to the street, uncoiling lengths of hose. They cursed Carter as he dodged between them.

A long hook-and-ladder rig braked to a halt behind the first fire engine and released more firemen.

When Carter finally got clear of the trucks, Espinosa and Ugarte were nowhere in sight.

"Shit!"

Carter ran to the next corner, scanning doorways to see if his prey stood hidden in shadow. When he reached the end of the block, he came up blank in all directions.

He took a deep breath, counted to ten, and let it out slowly. It didn't help. He kicked a garbage can and felt slightly better.

He went back to the fire. The crowd had grown so big that it filled the square. He saw Celia's blond head bobbing in the distance and started toward her.

Someone tugged at his sleeve.

Carter spun around, charged with adrenaline. He frightened the ragged ten-year-old street urchin who stood behind him.

"Señor Carter?"

"I'm Carter."

The boy held out a sealed envelope. "For you, señor. They said you would give me a dollar for it."

"Who gave you this?"

"The men who said you would give me a dollar."

Carter didn't have a dollar, so he gave the kid a five and took the envelope.

"*Muchas gracias, señor*"

"Who gave you the letter, *niño*?"

"Those men there, in the car." The boy pointed across the street at a double-parked car standing with its motor idling.

It was the same green sedan that had crushed the truckdriver earlier that day.

Carter stuffed the letter in his pocket and started forward.

A man in the back seat of the sedan waved at him. The driver beeped the horn a few times as the car drove away.

Carter rejoined Celia and Ramirez.

The fire was dying down. Firemen trained their hoses on the blaze, pumping torrents of water into the gutted shell of the building. A thick cloud of choking smoke blanketed the area.

Suddenly, the dying fire revived in a short-lived burst of white-hot incandescence.

"There go the autodestructs," Celia murmured sadly.

It was standard operating procedure that all of AXE's files and sophisticated electronics gear were rigged with fail-safe devices to melt them down into unrecognizable slag in the event that they were tampered with.

Ramirez couldn't take his eyes off the fire. He rubbed his blue-stubbed jaw. "Alfonso?"

"I'm afraid he was inside, too," Carter said.

"Tell me, señor, who kills like that?"

"Men—no, vermin—who aren't going to live very much longer," Carter said. "I promise you that."

"There's nothing more we can do here," Celia said.

They turned their backs on the charred ruin and returned to the limo.

Carter switched on a light in the back seat and examined the envelope.

"What's that?" Celia asked.

Carter told her how it had been given to him.

He weighed it in his hands, squeezed it, held both sides up to the light.

"I'm sure it's not a letter bomb, but it never hurts to check," he said. "Whoever this outfit is, they've had better opportunities to kill me than by booby-trapping a letter."

Hugo was unsheathed and used to slit open the bottom of the envelope. It contained only a folded sheet of stationery with some writing on it.

Celia asked, "What does it say?"

Carter held the paper so she could see it. It read:

> RAUL BOZA
> SITE # 195
> KM 53, NORTH ROAD
> CUZCO

"There's my next stop," Carter said.

NINETEEN

The torture house was located in a lonely place. The victims could scream as loud as they liked. Nobody would hear them but their torturers.

Ruiz hung naked from a chain suspended from the ceiling. A spreader bar secured to his ankles kept his legs open. He wasn't screaming now. He had passed out.

"Somebody give me a towel," Vasquez said. "The bastard got blood all over me."

"Here, use his shirt," another of the gang said. "He's not going to need it anymore."

Vasquez wiped his face. "Whew! This is thirsty work!"

"Have a beer."

Vasquez knocked the cap off a quart bottle of beer and drained half of it in one gulp.

"Ahhh, that's good!" He wiped his mouth with the back of his hand.

He and three of his men lounged around, taking a break. They were in a damp, dim, windowless stone cellar with a dirt floor. The room was lit by a single bare bulb dangling at the end of a wire, and by the cheery orange glow of a brazier filled with hot coals. The handles of long irons protruded from the coals.

The wooden stairs creaked as two men descended them: Leon Corona and Martin Santiago.

The torturers rose to their feet as a mark of respect.

"Has he talked yet?" Corona demanded.

"Not yet," Vasquez admitted. "He's a tough old bird, I'll give him that."

"He must talk! Ruiz has run with the Mesa Verde gang since its creation by Choey Montana. He may be retired from them, but there's nothing they do that he doesn't know about."

"If he's not talking, why are you sitting around doing nothing?" Santiago asked coldly.

"Because he's unconscious. Because he's old and we don't want to push him so far that he dies on us without talking. Does that answer your question, college boy?" Vasquez snapped.

"I'll bring him around."

"You like that, *compadres*? The big professor is going to teach us how to do our job!" Vasquez gestured toward Ruiz. "Go ahead, college boy! Show us how it's done!"

"I will."

"Shit! You should have done your job and killed the American. Then we wouldn't have to waste time with Ruiz."

"Why should I succeed where you and Yavar failed? Why didn't you get him?"

"Enough!" Corona said, silencing them with a curt chopping gesture. "Even if Ruiz talked now, I couldn't hear him over all your noise."

"Should I bring him around?"

"Yes. Give him a shot, Santiago."

Santiago took a leather-bound case out of his pocket. It was the size and shape of a brick.

"What's that?" Vasquez asked.

Nestled inside the case's plush black velour lining was a hypodermic syringe and a medicinal vial filled with clear fluid.

Going over to the light, Santiago filled the syringe with a quantity of fluid. He lowered the plunger, squeezing out air bubbles. A thin jet of fluid burst from the needle.

Santiago went to Ruiz. He turned his back to the others so they wouldn't see him gagging on the stink of roasted flesh.

He injected the solution into a vein in Ruiz's neck.

"What is that stuff?" a gang member asked.

"A stimulant," Santiago said.

"Why not just throw a pail of water in his face? That'll bring him around," Vasquez said.

"This will not only wake him up, it will prevent him from passing out, no matter what is done to him."

Ruiz twitched, jerked, moaned, and returned to consciousness.

"Back to work." Vasquez took a red-hot iron out of the coals and walked to Ruiz.

Five minutes later he admitted defeat.

"I can't get a thing out of him. If I push any harder, I'll kill him."

Corona squeezed Vasquez's shoulder. "You're a good man, Virgilio, but you lack finesse. These matters require a certain delicacy."

Corona took off his coat, and one of the gang held it for him. He rolled up his sleeves and selected a hot iron.

The others clustered around to watch.

"One thing you gotta say for the boss: he's not afraid to get his hands dirty," somebody whispered admiringly.

The screaming stopped when Corona paused a few minutes later. Ruiz mumbled something.

"Yes? You have something to tell me, Ruiz?" Corona's voice was gentle, caressing.

Ruiz's mouth moved.

"What's he saying?"

"Shut up, idiot, so we can hear!"

Corona held up his hand for silence. He put his ear close to Ruiz's lips. He concentrated on making out the words.

After a moment, Corona nodded and looked up.

"It's the Mesa Verde gang, all right. They're the ones who've crossed us. They're helping the American. Somebody's paying them plenty, but he doesn't know who. The gang is holding an important witness at a ruin outside of Cuzco."

"Boss, you're a wizard!" Vasquez enthused.

"Wait! He's trying to say something else!" Santiago said.

Corona lowered his ear back to Ruiz's mouth. He listened, frowning.

"What? What? Speak up, Ruiz! I can't hear you."

Ruiz's lips moved.

"I still can't hear you."

Corona moved his ear closer. Ruiz's head lunged forward. His teeth fastened on Corona's ear, biting it hard.

"Yahhhhhhhhh! Get him off me!"

Ruiz's teeth wouldn't let go of the ear. He was punched, clubbed, and strangled.

Corona wrenched free with a sob. "My ear, my ear! He's bitten through my ear!"

Vasquez's fingers dug deep into Ruiz's scrawny neck. "Filthy dirty bastard! I'll kill you—"

"Don't bother," Santiago said. "He's dead."

Vasquez let go.

Ruiz's head lolled on his chest. His bloody mouth was twisted into a wicked grin.

TWENTY

A few hours after sunrise, a battered old pickup truck passed the fifty-kilometer marker on a rutted dirt road north of Cuzco.

The road wound through deep valleys shadowed by jungle-covered mountains. Thatch-roofed farmhouses were sparsely scattered throughout the landscape. There were far more Inca ruins than there were farms.

The road circled the base of a mountain. A branch split off at Kilometer 53, switchbacking upward to a rock shelf that jutted five hundred feet above the valley.

The shelf was bare of vegetation. A stepped pyramid and a jumble of stone walls and columns sat on it. Sharp morning sunlight glinted off a group of vehicles parked to one side of the ruins. There were men there too.

This was Archaeological Site 195, but the armed men who patrolled it weren't archaeologists.

The pickup drove out of the shadows and into the sunny slope of a high western pass.

A curve in the road took the pickup out of the sight lines of the sentries on the hill. The truck slowed to a few miles per hour.

Two men rode inside the truck cab, the driver and his passenger.

The passenger was dressed like a peasant, a poor farmer. A floppy-brimmed hat shadowed his face. He wore a long-sleeved blue shirt and baggy dark trousers secured by a knotted rope belt. Slung by a strap over his shoulder was a bulky burlap sack.

His sneakers and heavy socks provided a jarring note, but they were necessary for moving through the jungle.

The truck eased almost to a halt.

"*Adiós*," the passenger said. "And thanks for the ride."

"*Vaya con Dios,*" replied the driver.

The rider opened the door, hopped out, and vanished into the brush crowding the roadside.

Nick Carter crouched under cover, listening to the pickup drive away.

Carter never walked blindly into anything. This setup demanded careful reconnoitering.

The driver was a farmer who'd unloaded his wares in the cold gray predawn light in the Cuzco marketplace. His return trip would take him where Carter wanted to go.

Carter bought a ride. The farmer was amused by the disguise but asked no questions.

He knew the site, too. The jungle surrounding it was honeycombed with trails. He'd delivered Carter to one of them and then sped on his way with money in his pocket.

Time passed while Carter waited to see if anyone had detected his covert approach.

No one came to investigate, so he assumed he had gotten away with it.

It was best to move now, before the sun got too high and too hot. Carter started up the trail.

The foliage was incredibly lush, nurtured by rain clouds from the Amazon basin. Trees hung over the trail, filtering clear light through emerald green boughs.

The ever-steepening trail twisted and turned so that no more than a few dozen yards of it were visible at any one time.

The forest teemed with life: birds, lizards, monkeys, and bugs. Vines as thick as a man's arm sprouted pink and purple blossoms as big as dinner plates. Huge white butterflies flitted from flower to flower.

Carter wasn't lulled by the idyllic setting. He moved carefully, constantly on the alert for trip wires, dead-falls, and booby traps.

He hadn't found any so far, but every bend in the trail might hide a deathtrap.

Sweat soaked his clothes before he'd been climbing too long. The shoulder rig concealed under his shirt chafed his bare skin with its straps. He'd cut a long vertical slit down the left side of the shirt to provide easy access to his gun.

The going was slow. The sun was nearing its zenith when the trail leveled out on a ridge. Carter glimpsed blue sky between the trees.

He pulled a pair of binoculars from his sack, hung the strap around his neck, and climbed a tree to see where he was.

The ridge looked down on the rock shelf and its ruins. A stone house stood to one side of the ruins. Near it was a flat dirt patch with two pickup trucks and a jeep parked on it.

A lone sentry was posted on top of the Inca pyramid, commanding a sweeping view of the valley below. He never once looked behind him, at the ridge where Carter was.

Eight men sat in the shade, smoking, drinking, chatting. Every man was armed with a pistol, and most of them had rifles as well.

Carter couldn't do much while it was light. He climbed down from the tree and took his lunch out of the sack. He unwrapped and ate his sandwiches, washing them down with sips of warm water from his canteen.

The hot sun made him drowsy. He curled up at the base of the tree, covered his eyes with his hat, and took a siesta.

Sound carried a long way in the high, thin air. The noise of a vehicle being driven at a high speed jarred Carter from his light sleep.

He climbed to his vantage point in the tree to investigate.

The men at the site had stopped relaxing. They watched a car that climbed the steep hill. It kicked up a cloud of dust as it zipped through the sharp turns.

Carter wasn't surprised to see that it was the green sedan.

It crested the road and slid to a stop on the level ground. Its doors were flung open and its riders piled out.

Carter trained his field glasses on them. He recognized some of the men he'd first seen in Lima. The sedan was in appreciably worse shape, which was to be expected for a car that had made the four-hundred-mile trip over some of the worst roads in the world.

The new arrivals were wildly excited. They waved their arms as they shouted to their *compadres* at the site.

Carter guessed that they were delivering some piece of news—bad news, from the look of things.

The men were galvanized into action. Some of them ran into the stone house, emerging a moment later with shotguns, machine guns, and boxes of ammunition.

The men from the green sedan loaded up with heavy

weapons and got back into the car.

The other men filled the two pickup trucks.

The green sedan reversed and barreled down the hill.
The pickups followed close behind.

They kicked up so much dust that the site was temporarily lost from view.

The convoy exited the valley by the eastern pass. They took the south road to Cuzco and vanished from sight.

When the dust cleared, only three men remained behind at the site. One was the sentry who had climbed down from his perch on the pyramid to see what the clamor was all about.

Carter dropped out of the tree, shouldered his pack, and started working his way down the ridge toward the ruins.

The thick undergrowth slowed him but provided excellent cover. It would have shielded a small army of infiltrators.

The foliage lapped at the gray stone ruins. Carter broke clear of the brush, hopped a long stone wall, and darted across the ancient plaza.

He reviewed what he'd learned about the site. It had been uncovered two years earlier by a team from the University of San Marcos. They were forced to abandon their research for lack of funds.

The group to which the men in the green sedan belonged had since taken it over.

Big blocks of masonry covered the plaza. Carter dodged from one to the next, using the massive stones to hide his approach.

The sentry and the other two men were still standing in the same place when Carter reached the front of the ruins.

He freed Wilhelmina from her holster and waited.

He regretted that he wasn't close enough to hear what was being said. It might clear up a lot of questions.

More than fifteen minutes passed before the excitement died down enough for the sentry to return to his post. The other two men went inside the stone house.

The sentry was a tall, gangling youth with long black hair and a wispy mustache. He wore a pair of binoculars around his neck and a rifle slung over one shoulder.

He whistled tunelessly as he returned to the ruins. A narrow dirt path passed through a gap in the terrace wall. Carter crouched to one side of the gap.

The sentry actually passed by without noticing Carter. The Killmaster popped up and laid the Luger across the back of the sentry's head.

Carter caught the sentry and stretched him out behind the wall. He used the youth's belt to tie his hands behind his back. A bandolier bound his feet together.

Hugo sliced the sentry's shirt sleeve into strips, which Carter used for a gag. The youth would probably be out for at least an hour, but the Killmaster took no chances.

He stretched the sentry on his back beside the wall. When he awoke, he'd have an egg-sized lump on the back of his skull and a king-sized headache.

Carter didn't like to leave weapons lying around loose. He unloaded the sentry's rifle and pitched it into the brush where it was lost from sight.

A big square window gaped in the rear wall of the stone house. There was no glass in it, but netting had been stretched over it to keep the insects out.

Carter watched the window for a while. Figures occasionally moved past it, but none of them glanced outside.

He wouldn't risk outlining himself against the sky. He dropped to his belly and crawled from the wall to the jeep parked near the house.

He felt every pebble beneath him.

He crouched behind the jeep. The front of the house faced the road. A small arched window was set high in the wall to one side of the wooden door.

He was still calculating his final approach when the door opened and a man stepped out.

He was big, tough, and hard-nosed. The bandoliers crisscrossing his chest and the twin sidearms holstered at his hips made him look like an old-time bandit.

He walked a few paces from the house, opened his fly, and relieved himself on a bush.

Carter almost hated to take advantage of it, but it was just too good an opportunity to pass up.

At least he waited until the fellow had finished.

Crouched low, almost doubled over, Carter padded up behind him.

The man was buttoning up when he felt the cold steel circle of a gun muzzle press against the back of his skull.

He froze.

"Silencio, muchacho," Carter whispered.

He pulled the man's guns from his holsters and tossed them into the greenery.

"You sneaky bastard," the man rasped.

"Shhhhh."

"Hey. Don't shoot, huh?"

"Not unless you make me," Carter said. "I just want a private chat. Let's go inside."

Carter marched his captive up to the front door.

"Open it."

The door opened.

Carter shoved his captive into the stone house and followed him inside.

•   •   •

"Take a look at this, Virgilio!"

The man who spoke was positioned on a slope across the valley from the ruins. Sunlight glinted off the lenses of the binoculars that he held trained on the stone house.

His sloppy surveillance technique would have betrayed his presence to the sentry had the young man not been knocked out by Carter.

"What is it, Pedro?" Vasquez asked.

"See for yourself!"

Vasquez fitted the binoculars to his eyes, focused, and swept them across the Inca site. He zeroed in on the image of a tall peasant holding a gun on a Mesa Verde gang member.

"Who the hell is that?" he demanded. "He's not one of our men!"

The gunman marched his captive to the stone house. For an instant, his head turned so that his face was revealed in the lenses.

"Can it be—?"

The pair disappeared inside the stone house.

Vasquez lowered the binoculars and rubbed his eyes. A huge grin split his face.

"It's him! I'd know that bastard from a mile off and this ain't no mile!"

"Who is it, Virgilio?"

"An old friend of mine. An American pig named Carter."

"Carter? Carter! That's the bastard that got Yavar! What's he doing here?"

"He turns up in the damnedest places. Well, this time he's going to wish he'd stayed away!"

"The boss said Carter was working with the Mesa Verdes. How come he's pulling a gun on them?"

"Who cares?" Vasquez shrugged. "All I know is that he's done us a big favor. What a stroke of luck!"

Vasquez gave orders to his *pistoleros*.

"We're moving out! Tell the rest of the boys to get ready! We'll hit the bastards now and wipe them all out!"

His men snapped into action.

"Carter!" Vasquez couldn't stop grinning. "I wouldn't have believed it if I hadn't seen him with my own eyes!"

"This'll cheer the boss up!"

"Tell the boys I'll lead the attack! I plan to give the *yanqui* a taste of his own medicine!"

Vasquez reached into his pocket and pulled out a hand grenade.

TWENTY-ONE

Diego was the man Carter had trapped outside the house. Maguay was the man inside.

Raul Boza was their prisoner.

Carter lined all three against the wall. He sat in a chair opposite them. He held Wilhelmina in his lap, not pointing her at anyone.

He didn't have to. The others got the message.

Carter enjoyed his first cigarette in hours.

Diego was stone-faced and silent. Maguay was more outwardly upset.

"Who the hell are you?" he demanded.

"I'll ask the questions," Carter said. "Where did the rest of the gang run off to?"

"They went to pick up some girls for the party," Maguay said. "But don't worry, they'll be right back."

"Good. I wouldn't want to miss them after the trouble they went to sending me an invitation."

Diego and Maguay exchanged glances. Comprehension dawned on Maguay's face.

"I know who you are! You're the *yanqui!* Hey, Diego, this is the one that Domingo told us about!"

"He didn't say anything about having my guns taken away," Diego grumbled.

"The *norteamericano* will give them back now that he knows he's among friends."

Maguay stepped forward, halting when Wilhelmina moved to cover him.

"That's close enough—friend," Carter said.

"That's not very friendly, not when we've been keeping this louse on ice for you." Maguay indicated Boza.

"Who are you?"

"We're the Mesa Verdes!" he said proudly.

"That means nothing to me," Carter said.

Maguay was amazed. "You have never heard of us? But no, of course not! You're a foreigner!"

"A stinking gringo," Diego muttered.

"Don't talk like that, Diego. We Mesa Verdes are patriots. We hate the Reds too. We've been holding this rat for you so you can hear what he's got to say!"

Their prisoner was in his early fifties. He was dark, balding, and fearful. His soiled clothes were of good quality.

Carter said his name: "Raul Boza."

"What—what do you want with me? Have you . . . have you come to rescue me?"

Carter didn't answer that question directly. "I checked your file, Boza. You were one of the construction engineers on the Apuchaka project."

Boza, agitated, shook his fists in the air. "That damned bridge! Always it comes back to haunt me! I wish I'd cut my hand off instead of taking that lousy money!"

"Who paid and for what?"

"The chief engineer gave me my share. He got the money from the higher-ups who were looting the project funds. I don't know who they were! You can kill me, but that won't change the fact that I don't know!"

"Calm down, Boza. Why were you paid off?"

"For doing nothing and saying nothing."

"About what?"

"About the bridge, what else?"

"I'm listening," Carter said.

"The corruption and graft was unbelievable. The contractors pocketed millions. Supplies were substandard. The concrete and steel were inferior—rotten. And so was the bridge. It was no good. I got down on my knees and thanked God that the Communists blew it up."

"Why?"

"Because the bridge would have washed away after the first big rainstorm."

"That's your professional opinion?"

"The Apuchaka span was doomed from the start. It would never have lasted more than a few months," Boza concluded.

"That's something you didn't know, eh, *yanqui*?" Maguay said. "We did you one big favor by keeping him alive, huh?"

"Could be," Carter admitted. "What are you getting out of this?"

"Nothing! We're patriots, like I told you."

"Don't believe him," Boza said. "They're nothing but a gang of cheap crooks!"

"Shut up, you!" Diego barked.

"Where did the rest of your gang go in such a hurry?" Carter asked.

"All right, I'll tell you," Maguay said. "It only proves I'm telling the truth. The Reds attacked our headquarters in Cuzco. Our men went to help out."

Carter rose.

Maguay and Diego shifted edgily.

"Hey, *yanqui*, what are you going to do?" Maguay said.

"You have the keys to that jeep outside?"

"*Sí*, but—"

"We're going for a ride," Carter said. "Away from here as fast as possible. That attack in Cuzco could be a diversion to lure your men away from Boza."

"What are you waiting for? Let's get out of here!"

He and Diego rushed for the door. Diego got there first and flung it open.

A high-powered slug hit him in the chest and blew out through his back.

Maguay flattened against the wall and kicked the door shut. Bullets ripped through it and ricocheted against the stone walls.

Boza cowered in the corner, hands covering his ears, his eyes shut. His lips moved as if he were praying.

A shout came from behind the house:

"Carter! This is for you!"

An object sailed through the netting on the window and hit the floor.

It was a live grenade.

There was only one way out and Carter took it. He dove headfirst through the back window.

The grenade detonated.

Carter hit the ground rolling and tumbled into a ditch.

It was occupied by Vasquez, who had taken cover there after throwing the grenade.

"You!" Vasquez shouted.

Carter still held Wilhelmina. Vasquez grabbed for the gun. He grabbed Carter's wrist and shoved the gun to one side. His free hand clawed at Carter's eyes.

Carter ducked his head. Vasquez's nails raked bleeding lines across Carter's forehead.

Carter used his head to butt Vasquez square in the face, smashing his nose.

Vasquez roared.

Carter got his gun hand free. He rammed the muzzle into Vasquez's ribs and pulled the trigger.

The contact muffled the blast. The muzzle flare scorched the dead man's shirt.

Carter rolled clear of Vasquez. He was sprayed by dirt kicked up by a bullet that tore the ground inches from his head.

Pedro stood at the corner of the stone house, angling for a better shot.

Carter abruptly rolled in the opposite direction, throwing off the second shot. Firing from the prone position, he shot Pedro in the leg.

When Pedro dropped to his knees, Carter shot him in the chest, finishing him.

Smoke poured out the window of the stone house. Carter hated to think of what the grenade had done to Boza and Maguay.

The shallow ditch ran parallel to the house. Carter crawled along it for ten yards, then raised his head.

Six armed men grouped in a loose arc converged on the house.

They were the advance team. The main force of the attackers was divided into two cars. One was halfway up the hill and closing fast. The other was parked across the dirt road in the valley, sealing it off.

Carter's burlap sack was in the house. It held a half-dozen mini-grenades and as many spare clips for his Luger.

The gun now had one round in the chamber and four in the clip. His stiletto was strapped to his right forearm, and the tiny bomb he'd dubbed Pierre was taped high on his inner thigh.

Except for Vasquez and Pedro, now deceased, none

of the advance team knew he had escaped the house.

Except for the ditch, there was no cover on this part of the rocky shelf. He couldn't reach the ruins behind him or the jungle on either side without showing himself. If the attackers just had handguns, he might have chanced a run. But most of them carried rifles.

He reached down into the front of his pants, freed Pierre, and put the mini-grenade in his pocket.

The jeep was fifty feet away, and none of the advance team was looking in its direction. They were focused on the house, wary that someone inside might have survived the blast.

Carter pressed the red button, arming Pierre. He broke from cover and raced for the jeep.

The rifleman nearest him glimpsed movement out of the corner of his eye. He spun, shouted, and fired.

His first shot was too close.

Before he could fire again, Carter heaved the little grenade.

He zigged and zagged like a broken field runner to spoil their aim. Bullets whipped past him. A shot kicked up a clod of dirt under his running feet.

Carter dove, rolled, and came up running in a different direction. He raced full tilt for the jeep.

The grenade exploded with a thumping noise.

In seconds, it spread a thick cloud of black smoke between him and the advance team.

They kept shooting but they weren't aiming.

Carter climbed into the jeep, crouching low. Luckily, the vehicle was too old to have been fitted with safety locks and antitheft devices.

Carter groped under the dashboard, feeling for the ignition wires. He found them and tore them loose.

A foolhardy type charged out of the smoke. Coughing, choking, half-blind, he fired wildly into the air.

He ran into a bullet fired by his own men. It dropped him but didn't finish him.

Carter's bullet did.

The Killmaster touched the exposed copper wires. They sparked and spat but that was all.

Another man stumbled out of the smoke.

Carter shot him.

The man was knocked down but not killed. He sprawled on the ground, writhing and moaning.

Carter made one last try at hot-wiring the engine. If it didn't work he was going to run like hell.

The wires sparked. The motor sputtered, coughed. Carter opened the throttle and the motor came alive.

He crouched low, raising his head just enough to see over the hood. He popped the clutch and slammed the jeep into gear.

It jumped forward with a jackrabbit start.

The man on the ground fired at the back of the jeep. His bullets scored a line across the rear panel.

The oncoming enemy car crested the hill and slewed across the rocky shelf on a collision course with the jeep.

Steering one-handed, Carter swung Wilhelmina in line.

The enemy car was so close that he could see the wild open-mouthed faces of the riders in the front seat. He squeezed off two shots.

One scored.

It punched through the windshield, drilling the driver.

The car went out of control. The man sitting next to the driver grabbed the wheel and wrestled with it.

He lost.

The car nosed downhill, lost its traction on the steep

slope, and rolled. It kept on rolling until it crashed into the trees at the edge of the jungle.

Carter holstered the Luger and gripped the wheel with both hands. He had one bullet left.

He took a wild ride down the steep dirt road, manhandling the jeep through the hairpin curves.

A big black car waited at the bottom of the hill. Five men waited with it. They started shooting before Carter was even halfway down the hill.

He wasn't going to run their gauntlet. When the jeep was three quarters of the way down the hill, he drove off the dirt road and down the steep grassy slope.

The jeep slid like a toboggan, nearly bucking Carter out of his seat. It came close to tipping over.

Then he was down the slope and on the main road.

The jeep bottomed out, stunning Carter with a bone-jarring jolt. The wheels dug in and the vehicle catapulted forward.

Carter drove toward the western pass.

The big black car followed in hot pursuit.

TWENTY-TWO

The pursuit car was a long, low-slung Lincoln Continental equipped with heavy-duty shocks and suspension. The weight of its five passengers provided stability and traction on the winding dirt road.

Carter thought he wasn't too badly off. He had a good lead and the jeep was built for this kind of rugged terrain.

Then he smelled gas.

The jeep left the valley by the high western pass. On the other side of the hill was another valley. A tributary of the Vilcanote River ran through it.

A small town and a railroad line lay on the far side of the river. A long freight train chugged down the tracks toward the town.

The smell of gas was stronger. The engine labored and knocked.

Carter looked back. The gas tank was punctured and leaking fluid.

The black Lincoln was gaining.

The jeep zoomed downhill toward a plank bridge spanning the river. The bridge was so narrow that only one vehicle could cross it at a time.

The jeep was ready to quit. Carter coasted down most of the way.

He rolled to a stop in the middle of the plank bridge and hopped out of the jeep.

A group of Indians idling by the train depot watched him curiously. A woman halted her pack-laded llama to see what he was doing.

The Lincoln was only a few hundred yards away.

Carter tore a strip off the bottom of his shirt and soaked it in the gas leaking out the back of the jeep. He unscrewed the gas tank cap and stuffed the rag into it.

The Lincoln was a hundred yards away and closing fast.

He fished his lighter out of his pocket and touched its flame to the rag. The rag burned fast, going up with a *whoosh*.

Carter ran across the bridge.

The train whistle hooted three times, the notes shivering in the valley air.

The Lincoln braked to a stop at the bridge.

The fire reached the gas tank. There wasn't enough fuel left for a big explosion, but the blast was enough to set the jeep ablaze.

Somebody in the Lincoln shouted that they should smash their way through the bonfire, but wiser heads prevailed. The riders got out of the car and shot at Carter.

Two of them were Ugarte and Espinosa.

None of them hit the Killmaster.

One of them tried to ford the river. He slid down the bank, holding his gun high as he plunged waist deep into the swiftly turbulent waters.

He got scared and tried to climb out. He stumbled on the slippery embankment and fell into the river. The current scooped him up and smashed him against the pilings of the bridge.

He was sucked under the bridge and out of sight.

The train pulled out of the station. The big black

coal-burning locomotive pulled a dozen hopper cars filled with crushed ore. The last car in line was a boxcar.

Carter ran flat out as it pulled away from him.

The Indians stared in amazement as he zipped past the depot. He sprinted on the ties between the tracks. He was losing strength while the train's speed increased. He couldn't keep up the killing pace much longer.

Then he got a break.

The train slowed as the road grade tilted upward around the base of a mountain.

An iron ladder was bolted to the boxcar's rear. Carter's palm slapped its bottom rung. His legs whirled in a blur of motion.

He jumped, grabbed another rung, and pulled himself up. He clung to the ladder as the landscape zoomed past.

The black Lincoln took the road that ran along the opposite side of the river. It passed the train and kept going.

Carter climbed to the top of the boxcar and lay flat on it, recovering his strength.

Five miles outside of the little town, another bridge crossed the river. It was an overpass that stretched above the tracks.

The Lincoln stopped in the middle of it. Its four riders formed a line.

Carter searched for cover. He was on the only boxcar. The hopper cars offered less protection. He could never reach the locomotive before the train passed under the bridge.

Carter crawled to the middle of the car. Safety handrails ran along the edges of both sides.

His plan to enter the boxcar ran into a snag: the door was padlocked.

Carter leaned over the edge and shot it off.

He holstered his now empty gun, grabbed the rail in both hands, and dangled over the side.

The gunmen on the overpass shot at him. They hadn't got the range yet.

Carter hooked the top of his foot under the door's massive handle and worked it loose, freeing the mechanism.

The heavy door wouldn't budge.

Bullets tore into the boxcar and whizzed past him.

The train climbed a slight incline. Carter's powerful kicks and the force of gravity finally freed the door.

Now that it was loosened, the heavy sliding door glided along the runners with guillotine force. It slammed wide open with a crash that shook the boxcar.

Carter swung inside and dropped to the floor.

The car was filled with tools and machinery. Carter took cover.

The train passed under the bridge.

Espinosa and two others leaned over the railing and unloaded their weapons into the boxcar.

Ugarte was nowhere to be seen.

A vicious fusillade sieved the boxcar roof. Carter huddled in his sheltering place, curling himself up into a ball to offer the smallest possible target.

The train crawled along at a snail's pace, giving the shooters plenty of time to turn the boxcar into a free-fire zone. They emptied entire clips, working their automatic rifles until they were red-hot.

But they didn't get Carter. He'd crammed himself into the central opening of a great block of machinery. He was protected by a layer of steel a foot thick.

Ricochets were the greatest danger. One of them took the heel off the shoe on his right foot.

One of Espinosa's men ran out of ammunition for his machine gun. Instead of reloading, he ran to the other side of the bridge, climbed over the railing, and jumped ten feet down to the boxcar roof.

Carter heard the thud of the heavy body landing above him.

The driver and Espinosa jumped into the Lincoln. The big black car went to the end of the overpass, whipped down a ramp, and took a road that ran above the left side of the tracks.

The train picked up speed on a level stretch.

Carter crawled out of the recess. The boxcar was strung with a cat's cradle of sunbeams streaming in through the holes that perforated the roof.

Footsteps pounded above him.

Carter looked around for a weapon. He grabbed a ten-foot metal pole with a hook on its end.

The man overhead lay flat on the roof, dangling his upper body over the side. He stuck his gun into the car and fired.

The bullet struck sparks off machine tools. Carter flattened against the wall and jabbed with the pole. The gunman screamed as the hook tore his hand, but he held on to his pistol and jockeyed for a better shot.

The door rocked on its runner as the train hit a downgrade.

Holding the safety rail with one hand, the man above thrust his head and shooting arm into the car.

Carter hooked the leading edge of the sliding door and threw himself backward, pulling as hard as he could.

The grinning gunman thought the deadly game of cat and mouse was over. It was, but not the way he expected.

The heavy sliding door rocked down the runner and slammed shut on him. He was torn from his perch and thrown from the train.

Carter waited until the train was on an upgrade before he opened the door. He didn't intend to get caught in his own trap.

The dead man was a motionless blot lying along the tracks a half mile back.

The Lincoln was much closer. It had kept pace with the train.

Carter had to take the initiative. He couldn't wait for his enemies to race ahead, block the tracks, stop the train, and hunt him down.

Maybe the engineer had a radio in the locomotive cab, or, even better, a gun. Reaching him would increase the Killmaster's options.

Holding the doorframe for balance, he jumped up and grabbed the safety rail. He got both hands on it and chinned himself up to the roof.

He went forward, crouched low with his legs spread wide for balance. He reached the front of the boxcar and got ready to jump into the ore-filled hopper.

A hand reached up and grabbed his leg. It tried to drag him down between the cars.

Carter's foot flew out from under him. He threw himself backward, kicking free.

He fell hard onto his back, which knocked the wind out of him, and he started to fall over the edge.

His hands shot out, grabbing the safety rail. The impact wrenched his shoulder joints, but he was able to hang down the side of the car.

He looked down. The ground was a dizzying blur.

Ugarte's head popped into view, grinning viciously.

When the train had gone under the overpass, Ugarte

had jumped down into an ore car and worked his way back to the boxcar.

Carter clambered onto the roof at the same time Ugarte did. Ugarte pressed his big booted foot on the back of Carter's face, grinding it into the metal.

Carter's fingers found a nerve pressure point on the big man's leg and dug in.

Ugarte howled as white-hot agony lanced up his leg, and Carter had the few seconds needed to wriggle out from under the boot.

The train whistle hooted urgently.

Ugarte lashed out with a kick. Carter bobbed his head at the last instant so the boot only grazed him, but it was still a stunner.

Ugarte hunched over him, legs spread wide. He flexed his enormous hands.

"No guns! I'll kill you with these!" He shouted to be heard over the frantic steam whistle.

Carter still had an ace up his sleeve. A twist of the wrist would trip Hugo's spring loaded sheath and put the stiletto in his hand.

Hugo wasn't needed.

Seeing what was coming, Carter rolled over onto his belly. He folded his arms over his head to protect it.

Ugarte thought that the Killmaster had gone mad with fear. Then he looked over his shoulder.

The locomotive and most of the ore cars had already disappeared into a tunnel.

The tunnel was low. There was barely three feet of clearance between it and the boxcar roof.

Ugarte was six and a half feet tall.

He opened his mouth to scream.

He slammed into the mountainside at a speed of fifty miles per hour and was brushed off the train. His broken corpse tumbled twenty yards before rolling to a stop.

The tunnel was as black as a tomb. Carter lay flat and didn't move until the train emerged into the sunlight on the other side of the mountain.

The train swept across a vast plateau. Its whistle shrilled many times, rising into a single sustained shriek.

Air brakes hissed. Metal wheels squealed against the tracks as the train ground to a halt.

The train stopped at a crossing in the middle of nowhere. A red pickup truck blocked the tracks.

Another truck and a green sedan also stood at the crossing.

The Mesa Verde gang had arrived.

The engineer stuck his head out of the cab to sound off about the obstruction. A gang member waved a gun at him.

The engineer pulled his head back inside in a hurry.

Armed men fanned out along both sides of the tracks. One of them saw Carter.

The group rushed toward him.

Carter looked back. The black Lincoln idled on a hilltop.

After a moment, it turned around and drove away.

TWENTY-THREE

"You're a remarkably patient man, Señor Carter. But then, I suppose that patience is the mark of a good hunter."

"It would have been a sin to spoil so delicious a meal with questions," Carter said.

The meal had been superb, a grand feast befitting the elegant dining room in which it had been served. Carter and the woman sat at opposite ends of a banquet table spread with snow-white linen. They finished up with exquisite little pastries and strong coffee.

Silent Indian serving girls cleared the table.

"We'll take our brandies on the veranda," the woman said. "Sunsets here are magnificent."

She was in her early forties and beautiful in a severe Spanish style. A silver comb pinned her jet-black hair in a knot at the back of her head. Tall, slim, and lithe, she was encased in a high-necked, long-sleeved black dress. Her lips and fingernails were bright red.

She was the former Dolores de la Parra, mistress of the hacienda outside Cuzco where the Mesa Verdes had taken Carter.

She and Carter went outside.

The hacienda was set high in the hills. A magnificent old structure, it dominated endless acres of terraced land that fell to the valley far below.

The crisp, clear air chilled fast now that the sun was low. The cool orange globe sank behind the hills.

Indians in brightly colored knit hats trudged across the landscape, herding a flock of llamas into a stone-walled pen for the night.

Carter was struck by the timeless quality and alien beauty of the scene.

A jarring note was provided by the armed guards patrolling the grounds.

"I have been waiting for this meeting for a long time, Señor Carter. Twenty years, to be exact," Dolores said.

"Why not call me Nick," Carter suggested.

"I would like that, Nick. And you may call me—'the one who does not forget.' "

Carter leaned forward. "What won't you forget, Dolores?"

"Colonel Edwin Dunninger."

"Why don't you tell me about him?"

Dolores studied the sunset for a time. "I was young and idealistic when we first met, full of foolish notions of doing something grand and heroic. The colonel was handsome and brave."

"You met while working on the Apuchaka project."

"Yes. I was a translator. I was raised in these parts and spoke the Quechua tongue of the Indians quite fluently. The colonel saw how useful that could be to his intelligence gathering, and so I became his agent. In time, our relationship became more than merely professional. We fell deeply in love."

Dolores sipped some brandy. "The colonel would have done anything for me . . . and I for him. In the end, he died for me."

"Why?"

"Not for the reason you expect."

"You vanished two days before he did."

"I did not vanish, Nick. I was made to vanish."

"By whom, and why?"

"I will answer all your questions, but you must let me tell the story in my own way. And you must do something for me in exchange."

Carter said nothing to commit himself.

"This is a splendid hacienda, is it not?"

"It's beautiful," Carter said.

"It belonged to my late husband. Since you are a foreigner, I doubt that you have heard of him, but Choey Montana was a name well known in certain Peruvian circles."

"He was some kind of a gambler, wasn't he?"

Dolores permitted herself a thin smile. "You are tactful, Nick. Choey owned many gambling houses, but he was no gambler. He was a poor kid from the slums who carved out a kingdom of crime for himself. He was a gangster and a killer, no worse than others of his kind, and better than most. His gang took the name of the first casino he ever owned: the Mesa Verde."

Carter got the reference. "Of course! *Mesa verde*—green table—the gaming tables on which craps and roulette are played."

Dolores nodded. "As I said, Choey was no gambler. He only bet on sure things. There was only one time in his life that he gambled on something. He gambled on me.

"Twenty years ago, he was hired to do a job of kidnapping. I was the victim."

"So that's why you disappeared without a word," Carter said.

"I was only a pawn in the game. I was taken as a hostage so that they would be able to control the colonel. I knew little of value, but he knew the truth about those who plundered the project. My life was the price of his silence."

Long blue shadows crept across the land.

"I told you that the colonel would sacrifice anything for me . . . anything. Even his honor. He corrupted himself to save me, but it was all in vain.

"The colonel died. Was killed. With him gone, I was of no further use to the plunderers. They ordered Choey to do away with me. He told them he had, but he lied. They never knew.

"You see, Nick, Choey had fallen in love with me. Instead of killing me, he hid and protected me. He even married me. Dolores de la Parra was no more. In her place was Señora Montana."

The light was fading from the sky. The evening star twinkled in a notch between the mountain peaks.

"I was a good wife to him, Nick. I made him happy. In time, I even learned to love him."

"Choey Montana won his gamble when he bet on you, Dolores."

"Thank you, Nick. You are kind."

Dolores sighed. "Most gang bosses are killed by ambitious underlings. Choey died a natural death, which tells you how loyal his men were. They have owed their allegiance to me since he passed away. I never called on that allegiance until the colonel's plane was found."

"You're the one who's been working behind the scenes."

"Yes. My country is ruled by an oligarchy of powerful and wealthy men. Some of them made their first fortunes on the graft they looted from Apuchaka. They are too strong to oppose openly. They went to work as soon as the plane was identified. They bribed Luis Chamorro to falsify the identification.''

"And then they killed him.''

"No,'' Dolores said. "They would have, but others got to him first.''

"What others?''

"Ah, now we come to your part in this matter, Nick. Two forces destroyed the bridge: the looters, and the Communists. They both will kill to protect their secrets. The Communists murdered Chamorro. When my information convinced the staff of *La República* to probe the case, they too were done away with.''

"By Espinosa.''

"He is only a hired hand. The death of Ugarte will hurt him badly, but beware—even though he's crippled by the loss of his partner, Espinosa is a dangerous man. Especially to you, Nick.''

"I know how to deal with his kind.''

"Yes, I believe you do.''

"But who's behind Espinosa?'' Carter asked.

"I will tell you, but first you must promise to do something for me.''

"I will if I can.''

"I want you to kill a man.''

Carter stared at her. Finally he said, "Your men seem capable enough. Why can't one of them do the job?''

"None of them is an AXE Killmaster. And there is another, more important reason. You will understand why when I tell you who must be destroyed.''

"Who?''

Dolores told him.

It was dark by the time she finished her explanation. A cold wind blew up, wailing through the mountain passes.

"One more question, Dolores,'' Carter said. "Do

you know who killed Edwin Dunninger?"

"Yes."

"Who?"

Dolores named the killer.

Carter shivered.

Dolores rose. "Shall we go inside, Nick? The night grows cold."

Carter's room was adjacent to Dolores's. It was spacious and handsomely furnished in Spanish Colonial style.

He lifted a curtain and looked out the tall, narrow window.

A half-moon floated in a purple-black sky over silver mountains. Moonlight gleamed on the stones of the courtyard. The rifleman pacing the square threw a long shadow.

Carter smoked a cigarette and stared at the night.

When he was done, he went away from the window and kicked Choey Montana's shoes off his feet. The baggy garments of his peasant disguise had been traded for Montana's rich, stylish clothes. They were tight in the shoulders and loose at the hips, but otherwise they weren't a bad fit.

A connecting door stood between the guest room and his hostess's boudoir. He heard her moving in her room.

He wondered if the door was locked.

Softly she called his name: "Nick?"

"Yes?"

"Would you be so good as to step in here for a moment, please?"

"Of course."

Carter opened the unlocked door and entered her bedroom.

A small fortune in antique furniture and objets d'art crowded the space. The sweet scent of perfume and cosmetics mingled with the aroma of fresh-cut flowers set in a porcelain vase. A full-length three-way mirror filled a corner. An ornate silver crucifix hung on the wall over the headboard of the oversize bed.

The sole source of light was a frosted globe lamp burning on the night table. The dimness was intimate and inviting.

Warm red spots shone in Dolores's ivory cheeks. Her shining eyes were demurely lowered.

She walked up to Carter, then turned her back.

"Will you unhook the back of my dress, please?"

"Certainly."

She shivered when his breath touched the back of her neck. The ankle-length dress was held together by a number of tiny hook-and-eye fastenings. She shivered again when Carter began opening them.

He paused when he reached a point between her shoulder blades.

"Don't stop," she murmured.

Carter kissed the back of her long neck. He put his hands on her pale shoulders and squeezed them.

Dolores put her hands on his and moved them down to her breasts. They were firm and full under the stiff front of the dress.

Her hips flared out from a slender waist. She leaned back against him, pressing her round bottom against his groin.

Her breathing became more rapid.

He took his hands off her breasts.

"Don't stop," she gasped.

"I won't."

He too breathed hard, and opened her dress to the

small of her back, easing it off her shoulders. She slipped her arms out of the sleeves and shrugged out of the top of the dress.

Carter drew the skirt down her hips, stroking her rounded thighs as the garment descended.

It fell to the floor and she stepped out of it and turned to face him.

She was laced into a black corselette. Its stiff cups arched and lifted her white breasts.

Her fingertips played over his face, neck, and shoulders. She unbuttoned his shirt, slipping her hand inside, caressing him, nuzzling his bare chest while he stroked her satin-smooth back.

"I have not been with a man for a long, long time, Nick. Tomorrow you will go your own way to do what must be done. But tonight you are mine."

Carter tilted her head back and kissed her hard on the mouth. The kiss was sweet and fierce.

He finished undressing her.

Her undergarments were intricate and exotic. It took time to free her from them. The time was well spent. He plied her with kisses and caresses that fed her hungry fire.

Black lace and satin ribbon rustled as the lingerie fell to the floor.

When she wore nothing but her glowing skin, she reached for the back of her head and pulled out the silver comb.

Great luxuriant masses of raven hair spilled over her shoulders and brown-nippled breasts.

Carter scooped Dolores up in his arms. She nestled her smiling face against his chest as he carried her to her bed.

TWENTY-FOUR

Dawn came to Santa Rosa.

So did Nick Carter.

He stood alone on a rocky knob at the edge of a cliff. The town was behind him. A thousand-foot drop was in front of him.

Santa Rosa, where it all began. Carter sensed that it would end here, too.

The town sat on a plateau three miles above sea level, nestling in the lee of still higher peaks. The thin air had a sharp bite. Carter huddled in the warmth of a fur-lined leather jacket.

The tip of his cigarette glowed in the frigid gray gloom. He flipped the butt into the abyss. It fell like a shooting star.

He was on his own, with no Mesa Verde men to back his play. They were out of the game.

Dolores had done what she could, but now she had retired from the field. She was a gadfly, stinging the oligarchs who ruled Peru.

The masters had had enough. They'd warned her that if she continued to defy them, they'd exterminate her and all of the Mesa Verde. And they had the power to do it.

Carter thought about how a handful of men could make a country their own private kingdom. It wasn't his

171

country, but maybe he could sting them too.

Sunrise over the snow-capped peaks of the Cordillera Vilcabamba was an awesome spectacle.

A man came walking out of Santa Rosa toward Carter.

Carter flexed his fingers, working the stiffness out of them. He opened his jacket and stuck his hands under his arms to warm them.

His right hand wrapped around the butt of the Luger. This time he had plenty of spare clips.

The sleepy little village stirred to life. Farmers came down from the hills. Vendors set up their stalls in the marketplace. Smoke rose from stone chimneys.

The walking man neared Carter.

"Do you know what the Indians call that rock you're standing on, Señor Markham?" he said. "Condor Point."

"Good morning, Quintana," Carter said.

"It's well named, don't you think? It looks something like a condor, at that."

"I hadn't noticed."

"I fear that Condor Point and the church are the only two attractions of interest that Santa Rosa has to offer."

"I wouldn't be too sure of that," Carter said.

"No?"

"You didn't come this far just to see the sights."

"Of course not," Quintana said. "I have a job to do. But what brings an American businessman here to the heart of the Andes?"

"I came to see the sights," Carter said.

"Most amusing."

"You don't sound amused."

"No? Then perhaps I'm not. You served a useful

function for a time, Señor Markham. You eliminated a number of troublesome fellows who needed elimination. That is why I allowed you a free rein.''

"You talk as if my usefulness has come to an end."

"It may be time to rein you in."

"It's been tried," Carter said.

"But not by me."

"Ugarte tried. He's dead."

"Oh? How nice. That only goes to prove my point, Señor Markham: you *do* serve a purpose.''

"Espinosa's still on the loose."

"I wouldn't be surprised if you ran into him before too long. He loved the big fellow like a son.''

"Like something, anyhow."

"Well," Quintana said. "I'm beginning to find our little chat a bit tiresome. It's been nice knowing you. Good day."

Quintana turned and started back toward town.

"See you later, Quintana."

"Good-bye, Señor Markham."

Carter waited until Quintana was a long way off before he took his hand off his gun.

Quintana disappeared into Santa Rosa.

The Killmaster had a hunch that Quintana was going to make a telephone call to a certain someone.

Carter ate breakfast in the town and then went to church.

Father Benito Jaran received Carter in the small, tidy office of the chancellery.

"Thank you for seeing me, Father."

"You're very welcome. Visitors are a rare treat here in Santa Rosa.''

"Not lately, from what I understand."

"Oh, you must be referring to the lost plane. Or the found plane, I should say. My, my, yes, it created a flurry of excitement here for a week or two, but that's all blown over now."

He gave Carter a sharp second look. "Or has it blown over?"

"Possibly not."

"May one inquire into the nature of your interest in this matter?" the little priest asked.

"Certainly. I'm a reporter for Amalgamated Press and Wire Services out of Washington, D.C."

Carter handed the priest his press card. Amalgamated was AXE's cover organization and his press ID often proved useful.

The priest glanced at the card and returned it to Carter, who slipped it into his wallet.

"I'll be glad to tell you what little I know, señor."

"Thank you, Father. I understand that it was just a freak accident that brought the plane to light."

"Some might call it a miracle," the priest said with a smile. "An earthquake opened a fissure in the bottom of Lake Quillacocha and emptied it. The plane had been underwater all those years. It was remarkably well preserved. The glacial water was rich in minerals that petrified the bodies."

"What became of the plane?"

"It's still up in the mountains, as far as I know."

"Were any records, logbooks, or personal property recovered from the wreck?"

"There were some odds and ends, yes."

"What became of them, Father?"

"They were taken by the government man."

"That would be Inspector Luis Chamorro of the Bureau of Aeronautics?"

"No," the priest said, shaking his head. "Another fellow took possession of the lot. His name is on the tip of my tongue. Give me a moment and I'm sure it will come to me."

Carter lit a cigarette and tried not to show his impatience.

"You know, I recall the official's name because it sounded very much like Lake Quillacocha, where the plane was found. It was, it was . . ."

The priest snapped his fingers. "Quintana! That's his name! Quintana!"

"I understand he's back in town now."

"He was very involved in the initial investigation. He's probably returned to tie up some loose ends."

"I don't doubt it," Carter said.

"He certainly did take an interest. A very pleasant fellow."

"Yes. What became of the deceased, Father?"

"They were brought down from the hills and given a decent Christian burial in our churchyard. I officiated at the service myself. No one has come forward to claim them. No matter. There's room enough for both of them here."

Carter paused. "You did say *both* of them, Father."

"Yes."

"Two men?"

"Would you care to see their graves?" the priest asked. They're buried behind the church."

"Why, yes, Father. I'd like very much to see them."

The priest came around from behind his desk. "I'll show you the way. I could do with a bit of exercise."

Carter followed the priest out of the chancellery and down a long aisle to the rear of the church.

They were intercepted by a tall gaunt man whose long

gray hair and full beard made him resemble an Old Testament prophet.

"Good morning, Father Benito."

"Good morning to you, Hernando. Say hello to Señor Carter, a *norteamericano* newsman."

"*Buenos dias, señor.*"

"*Buenos dias,*" Carter said.

"I can't polish the altar candlesticks, Father Benito."

"Why not?"

"We're all out of polish," Hernando said.

"There are some pews that could do with a bit of repair," the priest gently suggested.

"Oh. I'll fix them, Father."

"There's a good fellow."

Hernando shuffled away.

Noticing Carter's frown, Father Benito asked, "Is something wrong, señor?"

"No. I just have the feeling that I've seen Hernando before, but I can't remember where."

"I am sure you must be mistaken. Hernando has never left the village in all the years I've been here. He's served the church since long before I was assigned to this parish. He's a simple soul, one of God's innocents. And yet, who is to say that he's not happier than you or I?"

"They say the Lord moves in mysterious ways, Father."

"Indeed. Shall we go to the graveyard?"

Carter nodded. Still, he couldn't shake the haunting sense of familiarity that had come over him when he first set eyes on the caretaker. The question nagged at the back of his brain.

The priest opened the back doors of the church. The sun was bright and warm on the graveyard. The gently rolling knoll sprouted stone crosses and markers.

Father Benito led Carter to a pair of graves near the summit. "Here they are, poor souls. If they remain unclaimed, they may rest here until the end of time."

"Thank you, Father."

"You have seen what you wished to see?"

"Yes. You've been a great help."

"I am glad if I have been able to render some assistance to you."

"That you have." Carter made ready to leave.

"I'll accompany you to the plaza, if you like."

"Glad to have your company."

"I can do with a bit of leg stretching." The priest ruefully examined his paunch. "Perhaps it will help me work off the effects of Hernando's good cooking."

They walked around the church and entered the plaza.

The priest halted, frowning. "What's that car doing?"

A speeding car hurtled into town.

People scrambled to get out of its way. A woman snatched her child out of the path of the oncoming machine. It missed her by inches.

An Indian held the front of a two-wheeled cart loaded with chickens in crates. He tugged the rope, trying to move the cart in time.

He didn't make it.

The big black car didn't slow down; it speeded up, and swerved to clip the cart.

The spinning cart overturned on the Indian and pinned him under a heap of shattered wood and fluttering, squawking poultry.

Father Benito stared. "That driver must be a madman!"

The Lincoln roared into the plaza, its engine noise echoing off the surrounding buildings. It drove across the square, straight toward the church.

"Run!" Carter grabbed the priest's arm and hustled him up the front steps.

"But what—who—?"

"They're killers, Father!"

Father Benito charged up the stairs as fast as his legs could carry him.

The wooden double doors of the central portal were open. Carter and the priest ran into the church.

The Lincoln screeched to a halt on the cobblestones. Its front wheels nosed up the church stairs.

The caretaker emerged from under an archway holding a hammer in one hand and nails in the other.

"Father Benito, what's wrong?"

Carter shoved them both toward the rear door of the church. "Run! I'll hold them off!"

There were six armed men in the car. They piled out and charged the church. Four rushed the front and two ran around to the back.

Espinosa laid his machine gun across the Lincoln's roof and opened fire.

Carter threw himself flat on the floor and rolled.

A stream of steel-jacketed .45-caliber bullets tore craters in the church's stone walls.

Leon Corona crouched on one knee behind the cover of the Lincoln's front fender. His weapon was a high-powered rifle whose big-bore bullets could stop an elephant.

A fat man with a curly black beard worked a pump shotgun.

A skinny teen-ager with a red headband and a red bandanna around his neck held a machine pistol in each hand.

The quartet peppered the church with their heavy fire-power.

Wooden doors were hit, adding splinters and sawdust to the cloud of stone chips and dust wreathing the façade.

They did plenty of damage to the church but none to Carter. He sheltered behind a stone abutment, waiting for his turn.

Hernando and Father Benito ran out the back door.

Martin Santiago rounded the corner and came into view. He raised a sawed-off shotgun.

Hernando grabbed the priest by the back of his collar and hauled him back inside the church. The caretaker shoved the priest behind the wall beside the doorway. He slammed the back door shut and locked it.

A shotgun blast peppered the door.

Hernando was grazed but not seriously hurt. He ducked beside the priest.

A second blast tore into the door's heavy planks, spraying wood chips. Daylight showed through a score of holes.

Santiago broke the double-barreled weapon, extracted the spent cartridges, and shoved in some new ones.

The rifleman backing him up emptied half a clip into the lock, but instead of freeing the mechanism, the slugs froze it. He smashed the rifle butt into the planks, tearing them loose. When the opening was large enough, he shoved his hand through it and groped for the bolt.

Hernando pounded the clutching hand with his hammer, breaking bones and ripping flesh.

The rifleman screamed and fainted.

"Hernando!" Father Benito was shocked by the caretaker's savagery.

"The tower, Father!"

They dodged across the aisle and into the bell tower. The tower was a hundred feet tall. Steep wooden stairs spiraled up the inside of the square-sided shaft. A stout rope dangled from the bell at the top of the tower.

Hernando lifted the priest and set him on the stairs. "Up! Up!" he urged.

No mere locked door would stop Martin Santiago from making his kill. He set out to blow it to smithereens.

He emptied both barrels into the planks, reloaded, and fired again.

The door hung together by a few bits of shattered wood. Santiago blasted once more, and the door fell apart.

Carter had waited long enough.

The foursome at the front of the church couldn't keep up the fusillade forever. They had to charge.

The kid with the machine pistols wanted to be a hero. He shouted as he ran up the stairs, both weapons blazing.

Carter let him get inside before shooting him down.

There was a lull in the action. He didn't hear Espinosa's machine gun.

Outside, Leon Corona still crouched behind the cover of the Continental. He hadn't fired a shot.

He yelled at the fat man, "What are you waiting for? Go in there and get him!"

"Alone?"

"Espinosa's gone around the back with the others. The four of you should be able to kill one man!"

"I'm waiting for a clear shot," the fat man hedged.

Corona pointed the rifle at him. "I'll give *you* a clear shot if you don't move your ass!"

The fat man flattened his back against the church and inched toward the door.

"Move it!" Corona fired a shot near the fat man to give him some incentive.

The fat man charged. He held down the trigger and worked the pump action, laying down continuous blasts.

He ran into the church and tripped over the dead body of the kid with the red bandanna. He grabbed his riot gun and frantically whipped his head from side to side, seeking his target.

Carter was nowhere in sight.

A blur of motion at the opposite end of the church almost spooked him into shooting. He held his fire when he saw it was Espinosa.

Espinosa darted into the bell tower.

The fat man stumbled to his feet. Hot drops of sweat stung his eyes. He wanted to wipe them clean but was afraid to take his hands off the riot gun.

He nearly jumped out of his skin when he heard something creak inside the worship area.

Hiding behind a wall, he peeked around an archway. He saw rows of pews, the altar, the crucifix. He didn't see Carter.

A closer look brought an important detail to his attention. A gray scrap of cloth trailed from the bottom of the closed door of the confessional.

The *yanqui* wore gray pants.

The fat man grinned. He felt confident enough to pause to wipe the sweat from his eyes.

Holding his breath, he tiptoed toward the confessional. He stood facing it, unlimbered his riot gun, and pumped blast after blast into the wooden booth.

One burst knocked the door open.

The booth was empty.

Somebody whistled.

The fat man tried to look everywhere at once. He didn't see Carter reach out from beneath a pew and point Wilhelmina at him and pull the trigger.

• • •

Martin Santiago paused near the top of the bell tower to catch his breath. Running up the endless stairs at Santa Rosa's high altitude had left him breathless and dizzy.

He heard movement at the bottom of the shaft and looked down. Espinosa was coming up, too, but he still had a long climb. Santiago would have things wrapped up before the little killer reached the top.

Santiago leaned too far over the rail. The bottom of the shaft plummeted to remote depths. The bottom of his stomach felt as if it were going along for the ride.

Pale and sweating, Santiago crouched against the wall with his eyes shut, waiting for the spell of vertigo to pass.

Hernando crept up behind him and pounded Santiago's head with the hammer.

He hit him again and shoved him into the rail. The rail broke and Santiago dropped down the shaft.

Espinosa paused for an instant, watching the falling body, then resumed his climb.

Hernando ducked back, disappearing in the jumble of beams and braces at the top of the tower.

Espinosa didn't make Santiago's mistake of exhausting himself by racing up the stairs. The little man took his time, climbing slowly and deliberately.

He mounted the landing at the top of the stairs.

The top of the tower was open on all four sides. The light was broken up by the maze of beams and braces. A massive black iron bell hung from the thickest beam.

The space was thick with bird guano. The birds nesting there were upset by the noise and violence. They fluttered and squawked.

Espinosa squeezed off a burst at them.

A cloud of bloody feathers floated down the shaft.

A blur of motion hurtled toward him. Espinosa dodged with lightning speed. Hernando's hammer missed his head by inches and thudded harmlessly against the wall.

Espinosa smiled.

The priest and the caretaker crouched behind diagonal braces on the other side of the tower. Espinosa could have shot them up bit by bit, but he wanted to gloat first.

He stepped out from the platform, walking surefootedly on a catwalk that spanned the shaft. He paused in the middle, his back grazing the cold iron bell. He had a clear shot at the caretaker and the priest.

Carter entered the bottom of the bell tower and looked up. He was a top marksman, but the shot was too chancy.

Hernando tried to cover Father Benito by using his own body as a shield.

Espinosa savored the irony of the situation. "Say your prayers, priest."

"God forgive you," Father Benito said.

"I'll burn your church for a funeral pyre, *padre*."

Down below, Carter jumped up, grabbed the bell rope with both hands, and pulled down with all his weight.

The ponderous bell swung.

Espinosa stood in its way. It shoved him off the catwalk and into empty air.

Gravity yanked him screaming down the shaft.

The shooting had stopped.

The uneasy lull was broken by Espinosa's shriek and the thud of his body hitting bottom.

Somebody staggered into view at the side of the church. Corona held his fire when he recognized one of his men.

It was Victorio, the rifleman whose hand had been maimed by the hammer. Sobbing and moaning, he dragged himself to the car.

"Let's get out of here!"

"The others?" Corona said.

"Dead, all dead! Let's go! Let's get out of here—hey, look out!"

Corona turned to follow Victorio's fearful gaze. He bumped into a group of Indian men who had come up behind him.

There must have been two dozen of them. They were as silent as shadows. He hadn't even known they were there.

They weren't angry. At least, they didn't show it. Their flat, austere faces were expressionless. Their dark eyes stared right through him.

He had nothing but contempt for Indians, but now he was frightened. He tried to cover them with his rifle.

It was torn out of his hands. It hadn't fired a single shot that morning.

Corona pulled a pistol from his pocket. He backed into the car and waved the gun.

"Keep away! I'll shoot, I swear it!"

The Indians halted their advance but did not retreat.

A thrown rock hit Corona in the head. He jerked the trigger.

A man clutched his belly and fell to his knees.

Many hands tore at Corona. His wrist was grabbed and his gun hand was forced over his head. Two shots were fired into the air.

The gun was taken away from him, breaking his finger on the trigger guard in the process.

Corona screamed.

So did Victorio. They had him, too.

Corona fought like a man possessed but couldn't break free. "No! No! What are you going to do to me?"

One of the Indians said to the others: "Take them away before the good *padre* interferes."

Corona and Victorio were dragged across the plaza and out of town. They were taken to the rocky knob known as Condor Point.

Leon Corona was lifted high in the air by many hands. They held him spread-eagle under the sun for a silent moment. They were silent. Corona screamed continuously.

They threw him off the cliff.

He screamed throughout the thousand-foot drop.

Victorio went the way of his boss.

TWENTY-FIVE

Carter stood on the front steps of the church. He watched the Indians take away Corona and Victorio. He didn't know what was going to happen to them, but he was sure they were in good hands.

He extracted the spent clip and reached for a fresh one. He didn't get to load it in the Luger.

"You won't need that, Señor Markham."

Carter turned around slowly, holding Wilhelmina in one hand and the clip in the other.

Quintana stood inside the church, pointing a gun at Carter. "Mine's loaded."

"Your friends botched the job, Quintana."

"I'll set things right. And don't call them my friends. They're scum, criminals and Communists who didn't deserve to live."

"At least we agree on something."

"I knew you would kill them. That's why I told them where to find you. You served a useful function, my friend. We owe you a debt of gratitude."

" 'We'?"

"Men of power and prestige whose names would be meaningless to you. Men who wish to be spared the embarrassment of having old wounds reopened."

"Men who don't want their countrymen to know how they got fat on Apuchaka graft and then killed to keep their secret."

"Yes, those men," Quintana said, nodding. "Men who have decreed your death, Señor Markham—no, I shall drop the pretense and call you by your true name, Señor Carter." Quintana smiled.

"Why don't you let me in on the joke, Quintana?"

"I was just thinking how ironic it is. You came here to solve the puzzle of what happened to Colonel Dunninger. Perhaps twenty years from now, someone else will arrive to investigate the mystery of the death of Nick Carter."

"I solved the puzzle, Quintana."

"I thought you would."

"You figured it out too. That's why you returned to Santa Rosa."

"I didn't solve it right away. The two graves meant nothing to me until I checked the records and learned that there were three men on board the plane, not two. Three men. The pilot, the copilot, and the colonel. And only now do I know that the pilot and copilot fill those graves."

"Then you know what happened to Dunninger," Carter said.

"Yes. He must disappear once again. You will disappear with him."

Voices sounded inside the church.

Quintana jerked his head in their direction, then focused on Carter. "Here they come—ah, don't move! You only have a minute left. Don't shorten it by doing anything stupid."

"What can I do? You know my gun's empty."

"A most unique weapon, that Luger of yours. It will occupy a place of honor in my trophy case, I assure you."

"It's not doing me any good now."

Carter dropped Wilhelmina and the clip. He didn't

throw them, he just dropped them.

Quintana wasn't threatened by the action, so he didn't shoot. But he was distracted.

In the instant when Quintana's attention was diverted to the Luger, Carter snapped his wrist, springing Hugo from the sheath.

He threw the stiletto at Quintana.

Quintana's eyebrows arched in surprise. He looked down at his chest and saw the stiletto protruding from it.

He fell, dead.

Carter had kept his promise to Dolores and killed the oligarchy's top enforcer.

Father Benito and Hernando stepped outside the church as Quintana sprawled on the stairs.

Carter now knew where he'd seen the caretaker before. He visualized Hernando without his long gray hair and beard and minus twenty years. The face was the same as one he'd seen in the Apuchaka file back at AXE headquarters back in Washington.

The horrified priest asked Carter, "Who are you? What do you want of us?"

"I've come to take Colonel Dunninger home," said Carter.

The priest was mystified. Hernando blinked a few times in the sunlight. Then he smiled.

TWENTY-SIX

Brock was enraged and McLarran was outraged.

"You're finished, both of you!" Brock shouted. "I'll have your heads on a platter! You'll be lucky if you don't serve time in prison!"

"This is insane! Utter lunacy. The only charitable explanation I can offer is that you're both stark, raving mad," McLarran said.

"Shut up," Celia Rinaldi told them calmly.

Something in her tone got to them. They shut up.

The CIA honcho and Ambassador Sheridan McLarran were confined in a small room in the American embassy in Lima. A pair of crack marines stood guard outside the door. They were posted to keep Brock and McLarran under confinement.

"I had to send two of my people home in boxes because of you," Celia told them. "If it were up to me, I'd have you terminated. Unfortunately, you're more useful alive, but don't press your luck."

McLarran stared at her, white-faced. "Do you know who you're talking to?"

"Yes. Two traitors who've been selling out their country for twenty years."

"Don't say another word," Brock told McLarran. "Let them hang themselves. I want to see how far they'll go before they get slapped down hard."

Carter laughed. "I can't wait to see your faces five minutes from now."

"Oh, yeah?" Brock said. "What happens then?"

"That's when I lower the boom on you."

"Bullshit!"

"You're the expert on that score, Brock. You've been bullshitting the Company for two decades, but your luck has run out."

"Enjoy yourself while you can, Carter. You're finished. Extinct. I'm going to bury you!"

"Dead men don't always stay in their graves, Brock."

"What's that supposed to mean?" McLarran demanded.

"Let's go back twenty years," Carter began. "A band of Peruvian grafters got rich off the Apuchaka project. Their names aren't important here. They're the headache of the Peruvian government. What is important is that they couldn't have looted the project by themselves. They had plenty of help from the guys who were supposed to be on our side.

"Only they had a problem. They cut too many corners. The bridge was a catastrophe in the making. Once it collapsed, all the dirt would have come out in the wash. But if the bridge was blown up by Communist guerrillas, there wouldn't be any investigation.

"Time was running short and Colonel Dunninger's investigation was closing in fast. The grafters hired a local hoodlum named Choey Montana to abduct the colonel's girlfriend, Dolores de la Parra. That would keep Dunninger from blowing the whistle on them. They only needed to keep him quiet for a few days until the bridge was destroyed. Afterward—well, they could take care of Dunninger and Dolores.

"Dunninger agreed to play ball and certify that the

bridge was A-okay. Then the grafters got a lucky break, something they hadn't planned on at all. While he was en route to Lima to present his falsified report, his plane crashed.

"Dolores wasn't needed anymore, so she was the next to go. Choey Montana was ordered to kill her. She and the colonel were out of the way, and the bridge was slated for destruction."

Carter paused to gulp some coffee. It was cold, but he drank it anyway.

McLarran looked bored. Brock rolled his eyes as if he'd never heard anything so ridiculous.

"A hitch developed," Carter continued. "They usually do. The grafters got the bright idea of using the rebels to do their dirty work. They cut a deal with two top Communist agents named Vasquez and Corona. The boys did their bit and blew the bridge.

"That's where things went sour. Corona was the KGB's top local contact. He told his Soviet handlers about the deal, including the identities of the grafters who arranged it.

"The Soviets moved in fast. No way they'd miss out on a chance like this. It was a perfect blackmail setup: cooperate with the KGB, or be exposed as common criminals. Of course, once they started spying for the Soviets, our sticky-fingered bureaucrats weren't common criminals anymore. They were traitors.

"There were quite a few of them—traitors, that is," Carter continued. "It'll take the experts years to sort out the network of lies, betrayals, and treachery. I suspect that a lot of foreign policy disasters that were assumed to be isolated instances of stupidity will be revealed to be part of a deliberate pattern of sabotage and treason. I also suspect that what we've uncovered so far will prove to be only the tip of the iceberg. But we've got to start somewhere.''

Carter confronted Brock and McLarran with the full force of his cold eyes. They sat up and took notice.

"We've got to start somewhere," he repeated, "*so we're starting with you*."

Carter stepped back and folded his arms across his chest.

Brock and McLarran exploded in a tirade of abuse and denials.

Carter let them rant and rave for a few minutes. Then he asked Celia: "Had enough?"

"And then some."

"Bring in our surprise guests, please."

Celia exited.

"—sheer poppycock!" McLarran was saying. "A vicious slander and a smear tactic recalling the worst excesses of the McCarthy witch-hunts!"

"You'll pay for this, Carter!" Brock swore. "By God, you'll pay!"

The door opened and Celia entered. She wasn't alone. She was followed by an ivory-skinned woman in a black dress.

Brock and McLarran stopped shouting. They stopped moving. They could only stare at the dead past brought to life.

"I'm sure you gentlemen remember Dolores de la Parra," Celia said tartly.

"No—no! You're dead! You're dead!" Brock gasped.

McLarran turned on him. "Shut up, you fool!"

Another person entered the room.

It was Hernando. His hair was cut short, he was clean-shaven, and he wore a suit and tie.

"Dunninger!" McLarran rocked back in his chair as if he were having a heart attack. "It can't be! It can't be!"

Carter let the traitors look at Dolores and Dunninger for a minute.

He nodded to Celia. She escorted Dunninger and Dolores from the room. They left without saying a word.

Marines conducted Brock and McLarran to separate interrogation rooms.

The two men began their confessions. It would be a long time before they were done.

TWENTY-SEVEN

Ramirez and Celia drove Carter to the airport.

"What's ironic is that Brock and McLarran could have toughed it out," Carter said. "Dolores accused them both, but she had no corroboration. It would have been the word of a gangster's widow against that of a respected intelligence professional and a U.S. ambassador."

"Yes, but what about Dunninger?" Ramirez asked. "He could have backed up Dolores's testimony right down the line!"

"Why does a man like Dunninger spend twenty years of his life as a caretaker in a village church?" Carter countered.

"It's a mystery to me."

"Because he didn't know anything else. You see, Dunninger survived the plane crash physically, but not mentally. He sustained head injuries that left him with total amnesia. The local Indians found him wandering the hills and turned him over to the village priest who preceded Father Benito."

"Incredible!" said Celia. "But how did you manage to uncover his true identity?"

"It wasn't easy," Carter grinned. "When I first met the caretaker, I knew I'd seen him before, but I couldn't place the context. The church graveyard gave me the first clue. There were three men aboard the plane, but only two graves. Of course, there was no telling who was buried in them without an exhumation, but the fact that one of the trio was unaccounted for got me thinking about survivors. That same loose end was what brought Quintana back to Santa Rosa too."

"What clued you to the caretaker, Nick?"

"The man called Hernando had no conscious memory of his former life. But unconsciously—ah, that was a different story. When the church was attacked, the reflexes of a trained soldier took over and he defended himself and the priest in fine form—too fine for a mere simpleton. That was the tip-off that made me take a closer look at him and recognize Dunninger under all that hair."

Ramirez parked the car and the trio got out.

"One last question, Nick," Celia said. "Who tried to have Dunninger killed by sabotaging his plane? Or was it really an accident after all?"

"No, it was attempted murder, all right. Dolores found out the answer to that one."

"Who did it?"

"Buzz Kelly," Carter said. "The colonel's sidekick and best friend."

"Kelly—? But, Nick, that doesn't make any sense! Why would Kelly kill the man he loved best in all the world?"

"To save Dunninger from himself. Or so he thought. He knew that the colonel was going to perjure himself about the project to save Dolores. And once he did, the Soviets would have had their hooks into him too. Buzz Kelly was a simple man who couldn't bear to see his revered colonel betray his country, his honor, and his duty for the sake of a woman."

"Then Kelly hired the mechanic to sabotage the plane?"

"Correct. Buzz Kelly also framed an alibi for himself by picking a fight in a bar and getting arrested. When he was released from jail the next day, he rendezvoused with the mechanic and killed him."

"Incredible," Celia said.

"Most of it's supposition. There's no way to prove or disprove it. But Dolores was convinced. I can't forget what she told me. She said that she could easily have paid to have Kelly killed, but letting him live with his guilt was a far worse punishment."

"What happened to Kelly, Nick?" Ramirez asked.

"He hit the skids and the bottle. Drank himself to death a few years ago."

They fell silent, lost in their private thoughts.

Carter broke the blue mood.

"I'd better get moving if I don't want to miss my plane," he said.

He kissed Celia good-bye and shook hands with Ramirez. Then he picked up his suitcase and entered the terminal.

Celia and Ramirez watched Carter's plane take off. When it dwindled from sight, they got in the car and returned to Lima.

The Killmaster flew north, but not too far north. He got off at Cancún where a redheaded woman named Xica was waiting for him.

DON'T MISS THE NEXT NEW
NICK CARTER SPY THRILLER

THE POSEIDON TARGET

The bay door in front of the Mercedes glided up easily. He pulled the pins on all the grenades and started up the powerful little sports car. Then he stepped back and emptied the magazine across the windshield. The butt of the M3 did the rest and he had a clear field of fire from inside the car. He readied a fresh clip and started the Mercedes.

Just as he roared out of the garage he saw men spilling out the side window of the house. Two short bursts sent them diving into the bushes, and Carter put it to the floor.

Then World War III started.

The grenades went off in the garage and the gas tanks quickly followed. It was a quick-spreading fire. In seconds the whole compound was bathed in an orange glow. Men were running everywhere, firing at anything that moved including the Mercedes.

Carter drove directly toward the inner gate, the barrel of the M3 spitting slugs over the hood. When the magazine went dry, he laid it on the passenger seat and threw the last of his grenades.

If everything wasn't already mass confusion, it was now. About fifty yards from the gate, the Killmaster down-shifted and threw the wheel hard to the left. The car swung around facing the way it had come, with the rear wheels spinning, screaming for traction.

Out of the corner of his eye Carter saw two figures running toward him. By the time the face of one of them appeared at his side, Carter had his gun back in play.

The face became hamburger and disappeared. The second figure was in front of the car trying to bring an assault rifle up into firing position. The nose of the Mercedes sent him flying before he could get off a shot.

Carter retraced his route fifty yards, spotted the narrow lane, and cranked the wheel hard to the right. He bumped and jolted over the rough ground, twice bouncing the side of the car against trees.

He was close to praying under his breath as he hurtled toward the two trees and the trip beam. Already the wall was looming like a stone monster before him.

If for some reason the trip beam didn't work, he and the Mercedes would be an accordian against the wall.

He passed the point of no return, and then the blast erupted. He felt the shock wave and saw smoke and flying rock. For a second, he thought the opening wouldn't be big enough.

It almost wasn't.

He hit it at sixty miles an hour, and the scream of metal tearing off the sides of the car against jagged stone set his teeth on edge. Three quarters of the way through, he almost ground to a halt.

"Shit, shit, shit," he growled, and dropped the Mercedes into its lowest gear. The tachometer needle went crazy. Carter dropped the clutch when it sounded as if the engine would burst from beneath the hood, and the car shot through.

He turned right on the perimeter road and was through the gears by the time he hit the front corner of the compound. As he slid around the corner, he rammed a fresh clip—his last one—into the M3 and poked the barrel over the dash.

Twenty yards short of passing the outside gate he started firing, and kept it up until he hit the main road and turned left.

He discarded the M3 and checked the rearview mirror. They had the front gate open and two jeeps were already roaring through after him.

That was all right. He had expected it.

The jeeps would be no match for the Mercedes's speed. In fact, there was little likelihood that they would come anywhere near Carter by the time he hit Hong Kong.

But that wasn't the plan. The Killmaster wanted one more coup.

It was nearly a mile to the sharp, uphill "S" curve. Halfway through it, he braked to a quick, sliding stop, leaving the Mercedes sideways in the narrow road. Quickly he leaped out and plastered the last block of plastique to the driver's side door. He jammed an impact detonator into the glob and took off.

A shallow ditch paralleled the road on his left. It wouldn't conceal a man. Thin, scraggly trees were just beyond the ditch. They were bordered by a few low bushes displaying tiny, withered yellow blossoms. The other side of the road was even worse. There were wide-open fields without a ditch or a fence. The fields didn't look much different from the dusty road itself. It was a water-short, semibarren area.

The element of surprise wasn't going to be as much in his favor as he had hoped.

He started toward the spindly trees in a running crouch. He wasn't even off the road when the first pursuing jeep whirled around the curve, sliding to the extreme outside of the road.

Carter stopped, raised his arm, and sighted on the center of the windshield.

Just as he started firing, the second jeep rounded the curve, coming full bore.

It was made to order.

The windshield of the first jeep shattered, blinding the driver. It hit the side of the Mercedes full tilt. The explosion lifted the jeep high in the air, and it hurtled over what was left of the burning Mercedes.

The second jeep's driver tried to evade, but it was too late. He hit the front of the Mercedes, went up to teeter on two wheels, and then slid into the open field on its side.

Carter emptied the rest of his gun's drum magazine at anything that moved in or around the jeep, and took off.

If any of them were still alive and not crippled, there would be no fight left or taste for further pursuit.

—From THE POSEIDON TARGET
A New Nick Carter Spy Thriller
From Jove in December 1987